T0085804

PRAISE FOR

Article 353

"Sharp and memorable... a dark fable that reads like one of Georges Simenon's *romans durs* or psychological novels, which winningly fuse together lean prose, queasy atmospherics, raw emotion, and moral conundrums... [Viel] satisfies with a potent concoction of mystery, complexity, and tightly coiled tension."

—*Minneapolis Star Tribune*

"Mesmerizing and powerful... a biting social drama, a gripping psychological thriller, and an incisive morality tale... elegantly written, there is a beautiful simplicity of style that makes this so readable you will probably want to devour it in one sitting." —*NB*

"[A] beguiling noir...Arresting metaphors enliven the spare prose...Viel should win new American fans with this elegant effort." —*Publishers Weekly*

"Fresh and absorbing...grippingly told."

—*Library Journal*

"A surgically slim masterpiece...everything crime fiction used to be and ought to be...a brilliant story."

—*Durango Telegraph*

"A spare and lyrical tale of revenge and injustice."

—*CrimeReads*, 14 Crime Novels to Read This Month

"[*Article 353*] reads effortlessly and grippingly...an exceptionally well-written novel that completely and easily sucks the reader in." —*Complete Review*

"A subtle interrogation of the ways justice is conceived of and delivered." —*Ploughshares*

THE GIRL YOU CALL

ALSO BY TANGUY VIEL

The Absolute Perfection of Crime

Beyond Suspicion

The Disappearance of Jim Sullivan

Article 353

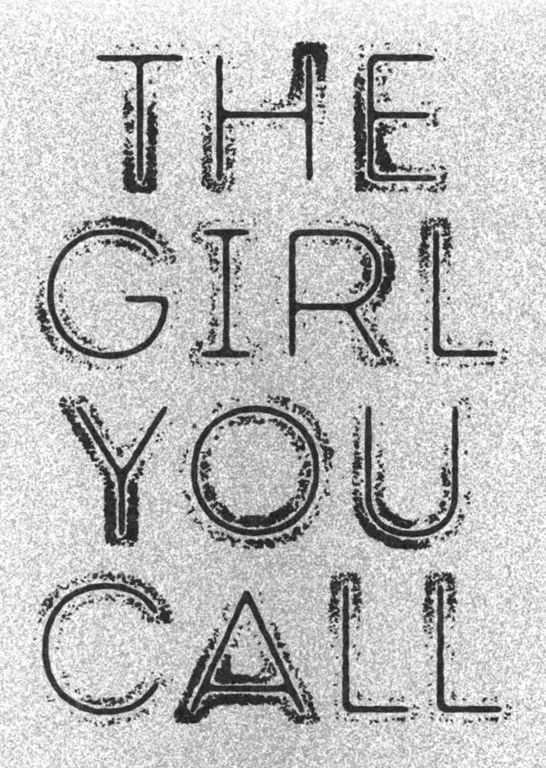

THE GIRL YOU CALL

TANGUY VIEL

Translated from the French by William Rodarmor

OTHER PRESS / NEW YORK

Originally published in French as *La fille qu'on appelle* in 2021
by Les Éditions de Minuit, 7, rue Bernard-Palissy, 75006 Paris.

Copyright © 2021 by Les Éditions de Minuit
Translation copyright © 2024 by William Rodarmor

Production editor: Yvonne E. Cárdenas
Text designer: Jennifer Daddio
This book was set in Goudy Old Style and Intro Rust G
by Alpha Design & Composition of Pittsfield, NH

1 3 5 7 9 10 8 6 4 2

All rights reserved. No part of this publication may be reproduced
or transmitted in any form or by any means, electronic or mechanical, including
photocopying, recording, or by any information storage and retrieval system, without
written permission from Other Press LLC, except in the case of brief quotations in
reviews for inclusion in a magazine, newspaper, or broadcast. Printed in the
United States of America on acid-free paper. For information write to
Other Press LLC, 267 Fifth Avenue, 6th Floor, New York, NY 10016.
Or visit our Web site: www.otherpress.com

Library of Congress Cataloging-in-Publication Data
Names: Viel, Tanguy, author. | Rodarmor, William, translator.
Title: The girl you call : a novel / Tanguy Viel ; translated from the French
by William Rodarmor.
Other titles: Fille qu'on appelle. English
Description: New York : Other Press, 2024.
Identifiers: LCCN 2023031770 (print) | LCCN 2023031771 (ebook) |
ISBN 9781635423259 (paperback) | ISBN 9781635423266 (ebook)
Subjects: LCSH: Boxers (Sports)—Fiction. | Fathers and daughters—Fiction. |
LCGFT: Noir fiction. | Social problem fiction. | Novels.
Classification: LCC PQ2682.I316 F55 2024 (print) | LCC PQ2682.I316 (ebook) |
DDC 843/.914—dc23/eng/20230915
LC record available at https://lccn.loc.gov/2023031770
LC ebook record available at https://lccn.loc.gov/2023031771

Publisher's Note
This is a work of fiction. Names, characters, places, and
incidents either are the product of the author's imagination
or are used fictitiously, and any resemblance to actual persons,
living or dead, events, or locales is entirely coincidental.

PART ONE

1

Nobody asked how she was dressed that morning, but she made a point of telling them anyway, that her white sneakers were the only shoes she had, that since dawn she'd been thinking about which skirt or jeans would suit the occasion, likewise which bright red lipstick to wear. She was sitting on the Univers Café terrasse on the big pedestrian square in the heart of the old city. Behind her, the words CITY HALL in very big letters could be read on the high stone wall, higher even than the tricolor flag drowsing in the warm air like a sleeping guard. Soon she would pass through the wide gate and cross the paved courtyard that led to the château, or what used to be the château, as it had long since been turned into city hall, though she would say it was all the same to her. In her mind, it made no difference whether she was meeting the mayor of the city or the lord of the village. She felt the same agitation and the same tightness around her heart at going into the great hall, which she was entering for the first time, almost surprised to have the automatic doors open at her approach, as if she expected to see a drawbridge come down across the moats and be dealing with a soldier in chain mail instead of a black-clad security guard. That's the way it is in this city, you would think the centuries had washed over the stones without ever changing them, any more than the sea did, which twice a day attacked them and twice a day gave up and retreated in defeat, like a dog with its tail down.

Laura was early of course, sitting at the café with enough time to have coffee and read *Ouest-France*, or not actually read it but skim the headlines and the color photos, lingering on the sports page just the same, wondering if there might be an article about her father, the boxer. At the age of forty, he had just won his thirty-fifth fight, and the local press couldn't stop celebrating his longevity, not to say his renaissance. Yes, "renaissance" was the word they'd been bandying about now that Max Le Corre was back at the top of the ticket from which he had disappeared for a while. She would probably have smiled to see yet another photograph of him in the ring, arms raised, under a headline aimed at the future asking, "Will he walk on water again?" Then, noticing the time on her phone, she folded the newspaper, put two euros in the bowl in front of her, and stood up. She looked at herself one more time in the café's big window, feeling certain, as she would say later, that she had made the right choice, the black leather jacket that showed off her hips, over a tailored wool skirt whose weft the wind barely brushed when she tugged at it.

"Yes," she told the policemen, "it might surprise you, but I told myself I'd made the right choice, along with the white sneakers everyone wears when they're twenty, so you couldn't tell whether I was a student, or a nurse, or I don't know, the girl you call."

"The girl you call?" one of them asked.

"Yeah, isn't that what you say? Call girl?" She laughed nervously, having said "call girl" without raising a smile from either of the cops, one with his arms crossed, the other leaning closer to her, but both alert to every word she used, which they seemed to be weighing like exotic fruit on a grocery scale.

Laura picked up her story, about asking the guard at the entrance to city hall where the mayor's office was, without knowing that he, the guard, would remain motionless and merely nod toward the big desk at the end of the hall, while almost automatically letting his eyes drift down her body from top to bottom. She was used to that, having men's eyes linger on her, and had long ago stopped paying attention to it, for good reason. From countless earlier occurrences, she knew she was attractive, maybe because of her tall stature or her olive skin, but in any case she had long been aware of it, and was indifferent to whatever charm she was exercising that day, neither more nor less, with her tailored skirt that didn't cover her knees, and the white sneakers that weren't actually white anymore because of their scuffed leather uppers.

At the reception desk, she again said that she had an appointment with the mayor, feeling sorry that no one asked her the reason for her visit, to which she would've said that it was personal. "It's true," she told the cops, "I would've liked it if someone had asked me, just so I could answer, 'It's personal.'" But nobody asked the reason for her visit, not even at the top of the high stone stairway she'd been directed to, not even the birdlike secretary stationed at the office entrance like an old crossing guard. The woman displayed the appropriate censure or envy while staring at her, if that's the right word, staring, her gaze this time falling like a guillotine from Laura's head to her feet.

Said secretary sighed a little, like the housekeeper of a great house who feels entitled to judge her master's visitors, then deigned to stand up and crack open a heavy wooden door whose passage she seemed to be guarding. She put her head in the opening and said, "Your appointment is here." Laura heard a man's voice answer, "Yes, thank you," and the old secretary invited her to squeeze through the opening, that is, through the narrow passage she'd deliberately left between the door and the wall, as if Laura, the younger of the two, had to push her way in, at least that was the impression that stayed with her for a long time. "Yeah, it was something like that," she said. "That I was the one who entered and not that I had been let in. But I swear I would have shoved her aside, if I'd had to."

And maybe because of the suddenly dubious look from the policemen facing her, she felt she should add, "Remember, I grew up around boxing rings."

They must have felt then that some part of her story lay in that sentence, pointing to the roughness of her childhood while hinting at the abyss that separated her from the man with the huge office, that nothing, neither the secretary's cold greeting nor the outsized room, had any connection with her own world.

"No, nothing," she told the policemen. "In a normal world we never would have met."

"A normal world?" they asked. "What would you call a normal world?"

"I don't know, a world where everybody stays in their place."

And as she tried to imagine that world, normal and fixed, where everybody had a maximum range of motion, like a mechanical figurine, her eyes wandered to the blue cloth of the jacket of the cop facing her. Expressing a thought that rose from deep inside her, she said, "My father seemed so attached to that."

2

Maybe I should have started this story with him, the boxer, since I can't say which of the two, Max or Laura, justified it more than the other. I do know that without him, she would certainly never have gone to city hall, much less entered the mayor's office like a budding flower, for the good reason that it was he, her father, who had asked for the appointment, first insisting on it to her and then insisting to the mayor himself, whose chauffeur he was. Max had been driving Le Bars around the city for the last three years, and they were beginning to know each other. The mayor was about ten years older than his driver, who flashed him a daily smile through the rearview mirror, or not really a smile but a perennial crinkling of the eyes. Max was forever trying to catch the eye of the man in the back, who often paid him no attention, instead looking at the slowly passing buildings and illuminated windows as if, because he was the city's mayor, he owed it to sweep his gaze across all the buildings and the people on the sidewalks, as if they belonged to him. His being reelected a few months earlier, after virtually crushing his opponents in the first round of the election, certainly hadn't helped foster a humility he already didn't have in excess, or at least never made into a cardinal value, being more inclined to see his success as the incarnation of his own tenacity, coming up with words like "courage" or "merit" or "work" to drop at random into the thousands of speeches he'd given during the last six years at groundbreakings and in television studios. You could never tell how much of this stemmed from genuine conviction and how much from self-regard, because you always sensed he was gazing beyond his listeners' heads, hoping his words might reach as far as Paris, where rumors were already circulating that he might be named a cabinet minister.

Max, who watched the mayor's face in the rearview mirror every day, didn't need a treatise on physiognomy to discern the drive and determination in it, under the heavy yet almost soft black eyebrows that contrasted so starkly with the cold, firm gaze that all powerful people have. In three years, Max had learned to follow its nuances and cracks, or rather not cracks but the deliberately allowed openings. If it's true that power is based not in rigidity but in the calculated placing of its inflections, it was like Stockholm syndrome applied hour after hour, where each time Le Bars shed some of his austerity, it caused a false tenderness to bloom in the eyes of his interlocutors, drawing them in.

By that yardstick, Maxime Le Corre was a good customer, as far as I can tell, like a grateful horse whose bit has been loosened, especially as he was burdened with the added debt he felt he owed the mayor, who had hired

Max when he was washed up—in the trough of the wave, as they say. Here is what happened in Max's life: First, a wave had borne him on its crest like a graceful surfer, then brought him down in its darkening shadow tunnel. For years afterward, both the luminous years he'd enjoyed because of his talents as a boxer and the darker ones that overshadowed them like a stormy sky would rise to the surface in his memory, like cutout silhouettes on a spindrift-spattered windshield. He had hoped to drag a heavy wool blanket over those dark years and leave it lying there, because of the long night without boxing he'd gone through since the light of the rings went out, blinking on and off even worse than a coastal lighthouse. This is something all boxers know, that the ring is like a lighthouse whose flashes you might count from the deck of a ship when watching for danger, and that sometimes you don't see the danger and get swept onto the rocks. This happens in boxing more than in any other sport: A boxing career has more striking chiaroscuros than a painting by Caravaggio.

When Max saw himself on billboards around town, he could hardly believe he was climbing back into the ring to box again, as he had in his glory days. Posters that sprouted like trees along the highways announcing the big bout on April 5 had photographs of the two boxers' bodies set against a starry background, fists raised and muscles tensed—Max with his shaved skull and his eyebrows already focused on victory, seeming to defy the entire city with his anger and coiled strength, above fiery letters that read "LE CORRE VS. COSTA: THE

Big Challenge." If you glanced at the poster and then at the man behind the wheel of the municipal limousine, you would have thought, Yeah, that's him all right, same broken nose and battered eyelids, same shiny scalp, the same guy who in a few weeks would be challenging the other local man who had long ago stolen the spotlight.

"It's getting close," said the mayor.

"This time two months from now, I'll be weighing in," said Max.

"This is no time to gain weight," the mayor remarked.

"Or to lose any," answered Max.

They talked about his previous victories, the great pleasure the mayor had taken in handing Max the winner's belt, the great pleasure, he said each time, in praising a real native, someone who trained right here, in front of the adoring audience, all so proud of the link that connected them to him, he who had always lived there, though in an unremarkable outlying neighborhood, some of whose glory was reflected in every window of every tower block where all the people lived whom he'd run into during his whole childhood, on benches in the squares, in elevators, and of course in the boxing gym whose heavy iron door they had pushed open at least once, and where they had all laced up gloves in the ring, imagining they were Mike Tyson for a moment. But of all the hundreds who had hoped in vain that some guy standing in the shadow of a column would see and notice them, the way an unseen god seemed to choose his prophets, only one had been lifted up, raised out ordinary life as it were, and that was Max Le Corre.

It didn't take a genius to see the uncommon power in Max's taut, heavy body, so it was also no accident either that one day a man in a white suit claiming to be a manager would enter the small gym where Max briskly dispatched his sparring partners and decide to take charge of his career, propelling him quickly to the national level whose title he would snatch. The trophy cup still reigned on Max's mantelpiece, engraved with the words 2002 FRENCH MIDDLEWEIGHT CHAMPIONSHIP. Fifteen years later and already aged, Max was amazed to still read words like "renaissance" and even "resurrection" in the press. Resurrection was the other word he would sometimes see in the newspapers, and he disliked it as much as renaissance, because when the two words were deliberately used, they created the same vacuum sucking him toward the abyss that had preceded them.

To the mayor, he said, "If you'd told me I'd still be boxing at forty..."

"They say boxing is mostly in your head," said the man in the back, still looking out the window.

His eyes on the road in front of him, Max pursed his lips ever so slightly, in a way that might mean, If I clocked you one, you'd see what it does in your head, but ever so slightly, so his silence was also acquiescence. The mayor was right, of course, boxing is mainly in your head, it's a sport of nerves and mental strength, yes, that's right, that was something Max wouldn't deny.

"Anyway, it takes guts to face Costa," the mayor continued.

"It's now or never," answered Max. "Time isn't on my side." And in this he was right, that boxing at his age, at least this is how he felt, was like skating on a frozen lake at the very end of winter. In spite of his victories, he wasn't fooled by the thin coat of ice he was gliding across, still unafraid to cut the most delicate figures, but resignedly awaiting the day when the ice would suddenly crack and he would drown in the too-cold water.

"You're going to win, Max. I'm sure of it."

Taking advantage of this moment when the mayor seemed to be on his side, Max finally brought up the thing that been on his mind for days, which that very morning when he got up he had promised himself he would raise, and which had nothing to do with boxing, no, it was about his daughter, he wanted to talk about his daughter. "I'd like to ask you a small favor, Mr. Mayor, it's about my daughter. She has moved back here and–"

"Sure," said the mayor. "Go on."

"It's that she asked for an apartment from the city housing authority, but you know what it's like, it takes time, and I figured maybe you could–"

To save him from floundering, the mayor cut the request short by saying, "Of course, Max. Tell her to come see me at city hall, and I'll see what I can do."

And as the car drove along the row of fully rigged tall ships like an open-air museum, Max heaved a sigh of relief, as if he had just left an exam room feeling that he had passed, even as he repeated to the man in the back that it was very nice of him to take the time to meet with her, that he didn't have to do that, while he, the man in the back, busy straightening his tie or brushing the sleeves of his suit, answered that it was nothing, that in a way it was part of his job, that he had been elected for that, to help people. Max hoped that it would go well, that she would measure up. He said so later, Max did, that he had thought of that phrase. "Yes, it's true, I hoped that she would measure up."

3

Did Laura measure up? You better believe it. When the office door closed behind her and she found herself facing the mayor, he couldn't help giving her figure that same plunging, vertical look. But she paid it no attention, struck as she was by the huge size of the luxurious office she had just entered. For a moment she thought she was in the Élysée Palace or something, because of all the old armchairs, the medieval tapestries of hunting scenes, and the heavy woodwork, the caissons adorning the painted ceiling. That's the way it is in France, where the ancien régime lives on in mayors' offices. He immediately got up from his leather armchair and made his way through the antique furniture to greet her and shake her hand, saying, "Hello, Laura! How are you?"

"Yeah," she said, "he called me by my first name, like we'd known each other since forever." Yet she'd hardly ever met him before, maybe once with her father, but he wasn't the mayor at the time and she didn't remember. Maybe he did that with everyone, like everybody was entitled to his smile and his use of their first name, a kind of goodwill he acquired along with his position so that there would never be distance between him and the city's inhabitants, citizens, constituents beyond that of the responsibilities with which he'd very temporarily been entrusted. In any case, those are things that Le Bars could have told her, word for word, maybe because nothing pleased him more than his feeling of condescending to normal life, assuming he saw normal life as the undifferentiated mass of people, the ones he himself called "the people." Since his election, his role was to know "the people," to love them, and to make himself believe that he loved them, unless—and this was also possible—he loved seeing himself in the act of loving them.

Laura, who was pretty levelheaded, would sense things like that, even though she'd been worrying since the night before about what she would wear and say, even if a part of her trembled like a child summoned to the principal's office, she was perfectly aware that when he got up that morning, he didn't even know his schedule for the day. And that's really why they didn't start off on an equal footing, she, Laura Le Corre, twenty, a student, and he, Quentin Le Bars, forty-eight, the mayor.

"A student?" asked one of the cops.

"Yeah, that is, no. Well, that's what I told him, that I was a student, that I was getting a degree in psych. It felt right to me, and mainly it was believable, because I've always liked psychology." She shifted back in her chair, and said, "That doesn't make it any clearer, does it?"

Instead of thinking how he could be sure of what she'd just said, the cop who was trying harder than his partner to understand her, trying to turn what she was saying into written sentences, with one eye on her and the other on his computer keyboard, said, "So you lied to him?"

"What? Do you think it would've been normal for me to tell him that..."

She stopped herself without waiting for the cop to interrupt her, allowing three long ellipses to leave her lips, as if she had lightly stepped away from her own words to allow him to enter her sentence. He jumped right in, saying, "That you would tell him what?"

It was as if they were starting to write a partita together, a symphony of hooks and mutual stresses, as measured as the words in an opera libretto—she, the elegiac soprano spinning out her lament over as many acts as necessary, he, a somber baritone in service to a diva.

"That you would tell him what?" he repeated.

She hesitated before answering, and the other cop, the one who had been standing near the window, now moved closer to the big table they used as their desk. He put his hand on his partner's shoulder, as if to tell him to take it easy, that they shouldn't rush her, to remember that she was the one filing the complaint. Sensing the turn the interview was taking, the cop on his feet very quietly said, "You can still back out, you know." It wasn't clear if it was encouragement or advice.

But as he was trying soothe her, maybe because she was the boxer's daughter, or some stubborn, restive animal, she said, "You're kidding, I hope?"

Stung by her comeback, the first cop felt justified in returning to the fray and bringing the interview back to the way he intended to conduct it. He said, "At least it's best to tell us everything, right?"

And that was true. It was best to tell everything. At least that was the best advice he could've given her.

"I worked in fashion," she said.

The two cops glanced at each other, exchanging the kind of male look composed of a strange mix they themselves couldn't identify. The expression "in fashion" suggested that they better keep an eye on each other, as if they could already imagine the dirty cracks that would spread like wildfire down the hallways of the police station. The exchange probably lasted no more than a fraction of a second, but it was long enough for Laura to catch it, long enough in that same extended second for at least one of them to feel unmasked. In his only defense, he returned to the charge.

"Why did you lie?"

"I don't know. He was the mayor. I had an appointment with the mayor."

She didn't say that in general she preferred to lie, that she had also lied to her father, that she'd come back to his place for that very reason, to lie and to change everything, the way when you're twenty you think that everything will be erased and forgotten by merely moving across a map of the city. But she had to tell the policemen what had actually happened, things she didn't want to tell the mayor, that no, she had never registered at the university, hadn't even finished high school, and for good reason: They came to find her there one day after class, approaching her because...

She didn't dare finish that sentence either, and the two cops didn't pick up on it, because at that moment all three knew they were speaking the same language, or at least the same silence, which carried within it the same established fact: that Laura was beautiful, and that her body bore all the criteria of beauty.

At least that was what they must have figured, the men who showed up after classes one day to suggest that she enter the adult world ahead of schedule. She was barely sixteen, but for the guys waiting in the parking lot, that was exactly their target and this was exactly their job, to spot pretty girls, approach them on beaches or in high-school courtyards, and toss a net over them with strands so fine that the moment the chosen girls said yes, even just once, they could no more escape than stray dogs captured by the pound. Laura was no different, walking along the fence outside the high school, no more able to speed up and tell them to get lost when they approached her, getting right to the point: "Would you be interested in working in fashion, miss?" She took it as an almost funny way of getting her attention, enough to stop and let them spin their web of friendly phrases, saying that if she cared to come with them, they could do a test, take a few pictures just to see, after that, she could do whatever she wanted.

Two hours later she found herself with four fifty-euro bills in her hand, thinking that if this is what the fashion world is like, then sign me up right away. Especially because she quickly figured that they would be free and easy with those fifty-euro bills, because to them, Laura was the rare pearl, the one you don't often come across, where you couldn't tell if she met the standards of the times or helped set them as irrevocably as the judgment of Paris in choosing Aphrodite. It was what made them say, "Yeah, that's her, today's beauty, she's the one." And it wasn't six months later before you began to see her showing off her body for this or that brand of underwear, soon appearing on posters on all the city's walls and big wooden billboards, every day drifting a little farther away from high-school life.

She didn't go into detail in front of the policemen, saying only that she'd earned quite a lot of money in a few afternoons spent in front of a photographer's flashgun, careful not to tell them that sometimes she had to take off that underwear and pose more lasciviously—and more lucratively—for the kind of magazine found on the higher racks at newsstands.

She didn't say that, and at the time it might not even have occurred to her, since she'd put it so far behind her, using that strange power that young people invent to convince themselves that with time, everything fades away and disappears.

"So you were a model?" they said.

"Yeah, sort of a model," she said. "That's right." And the look she gave them held all the anxiety she felt about exactly how much they knew, meaning whether they'd had occasion to see her smile or her hair on the big train station billboards, or even more.

"You must have run into some odd people."

"You know, to get a handle on things you can sometimes just stick to the clichés you might have," she said. Then, as if the thought had just occurred to her, she added, "After all, maybe it's the same thing for you."

"The same thing for us?"

"I mean you, the police. Maybe all the various worlds are just the clichés we have about them."

You would think this irritated the older of the two cops, maybe the more bitter or more blasé one, who was still standing backlit by the window, because what came out was like a dart fired from a blowgun he'd kept hidden behind his lips: "Photographs are one thing, but did it stop there?"

"What do you mean?" she asked, though she understood the point of the question, or rather the insinuation that he would have to clarify for her because she wasn't about to do it for him.

"Well, it's simple: Did you have relations with your employers?"

"It happened, yeah."

"And you never felt that you were..."

"What, prostituting myself?"

And she realized that she had just brought them up short, or at least kept them from saying the word they might've chosen instead of prostitution. They might have preferred to say "provocative." They might have asked, "Did you ever feel that you were provocative with them?" She knew perfectly well how delicate it was for them to go there. She only had to stay just far enough ahead of them so that they wouldn't dare backtrack or twist what she was saying, and that's what happened.

They fell silent, and she continued: "Yes, it's true, the first time that I saw my body in underwear on the city's billboards, and I saw my breasts spilling out of the lace and my smile aimed at all of you, yes, I can say I had the feeling that I had prostituted myself."

And in spite of her somewhat forced seriousness and the calculated theatricality they couldn't fail to notice, something decent or moral kept them from pursuing the point.

"What about your father?" asked one. "Did he know?"

"No. That is, I don't know. I don't think so."

And she didn't need to add, I'd rather not know, because in the time since she'd come back, Max hadn't once asked her flat out, never made her sit beside him and said, "We haven't seen each other very much these last years. Tell me, what have you been doing all that time?"

And for good reason: He knew, though he would've preferred to find it out other than by spotting her on advertising billboards, other than seeing her draped across the city's walls, while also glancing in his rearview mirror to ascertain if the mayor himself had seen the same thing, if he had been attracted by her hips or her eyes. But he, the boxer, said nothing, because of the shame and at the same time hoping that Le Bars didn't know, wondering if she resembled him enough that someone might wonder, or say, "It's crazy how much she looks like him, maybe she's his daughter after all."

Because then father and daughter might have crossed paths on the granite walls by the proxy of their posters, both nearly naked, their compelling gaze designed to attract attention, although the opposite of each other, each embodying the most archetypical signs of masculine and feminine—he a beast of muscles whose every vein popped with strength and virility, she all lascivious curves, white teeth nibbling her lips. They could have run into each other on the city walls, gazing at each other incestuously, as it were, but it never happened. It was as if an unusual system of communicating vases worked so they never caught the light at the same time, but alternately, as if a laughing god in heaven had aimed his only spotlight first on one and then on the other, in turn.

4

Le Bars could have sat back down behind his big mayor's desk and offered Laura a chair facing him, but he gestured to the leather sofa that marked a small sitting area near the window instead. "Come over here," he said. "We'll be more comfortable."

"I'll never know if this was special treatment," she said later, "or if he tried to put all his visitors at ease, making them forget the heavy furniture, which was only his as a tenant. Anyway that's what he said, 'I'm just a tenant here, you know.'" She was looking over the whole room, getting used to all that luxury the way you get used to the light when you come out of a tunnel, when he asked her to sit down. Only he didn't use the formal "*vous*." Instead, it was the informal "*tu*."

Laura acted as if she wasn't surprised that he would use "*tu*" with her so quickly, that maybe because she was so young, it was normal that he be more familiar with her than with someone else. And of course she was Max's daughter, and not only the great boxer's daughter but, more to the point, his driver's daughter. She sat down on the edge of the sofa, as if afraid to sink too deeply into the foam cushions. She thanked him for agreeing to take the time to meet with her, but he immediately interrupted her, insisting that it was normal, that if he could help her, of course he would. Still standing, he lit a cigarette.

"You don't mind if I smoke, do you?"

She shook her head.

"Help yourself, if you like."

He held the pack out to her, not doubting for a moment that she was a smoker. She would have loved a cigarette, but didn't allow herself take one. She looked at the pack several times, and later on, the cigarette pack would be all she looked at, concentrating on it so as not to feel overwhelmed. Le Bars pulled the ashtray on the coffee table closer, and sat down in the armchair facing her with the ease of someone who feels at home and knows how objects react, down to the slight rebound of the cushions he was sinking into. He propped his elbows on the armrests and leaned forward a little, as if he were growing larger with the light behind him and his entire body on a diagonal to her. Probably by reflex, she squeezed her legs together slightly.

"So, what can I do for you?" he asked.

With sunlight streaming across the floor and the old marquetry wood furniture, and the windows' latticework creating a slanting grid on the thick carpet, she finally said that she had just recently come back, that she was staying with her father for the time being, that she had submitted an application for housing, but that maybe he could back up her request, and that it would be wonderful for her if...

"Well, finding housing isn't easy."

He hadn't taken his eyes off her from the very first moment, diving in as if into a volcanic lake whose shores he didn't want to see, leaving her in her silence to wonder what she should say next, as if she'd been forced to be there and was now being made to beg for something.

"You know," she said, "I would never have dreamed of asking you for anything, but my father insisted that..."

At that moment Le Bars realized he had forgotten about Laura's father, and also realized that he absolutely didn't want to think about him now. He tried to restart the conversation any way he could, provided he didn't feel Max coming between them. Without realizing whether he was acting out of calculation or instinct, he asked, "Where were you, before?"

"In Rennes," she said.

"Ah, yes, Rennes. Rennes is nice, it's young and lively. But at your age, leaving Rennes to come here... It's usually the other way around, isn't it?"

She didn't know whether she should answer yes or no, because of everything she didn't want to bring up of her earlier life, and which had been rising more clearly in her memory these last days, like a dead skin she wasn't able to slough off that held all those things in faded images, not worn or outdated but more like memories in gestation, as if they hadn't spent enough time in the chemical bath of memory for the clearest shapes and colors to develop.

"Yeah, that's probably right," she finally said.

She explained that she now wanted to make her life here in the city where she was born and which she had left so long ago—what, six or seven years?—that she had sometimes come back to see her father, but that since she and her mother had basically fled from the family home, she had never spent more than a weekend in her hometown.

"And also... I missed the sea."

"Ah, the sea," he said. "No shortage of that around here. What are you doing right now? I mean, do you have a job?"

"No, not yet," she said. "I'm looking..."

"In what area, psychology?"

She couldn't tell if there was sarcasm or defiance in the question, but she finally answered, "Not necessarily. Pretty much anything."

He stood up from his armchair as he asked the question, as if he suddenly wanted to cut the meeting short. For a moment, she thought he was annoyed. He walked to the big windows overlooking the courtyard with his hands in his pants pockets, his wrists pushing the hem of his jacket up. He stood for a long moment with his back to her, before half turning around to her somewhat quickly, somewhat nervously too, like someone starting down an unknown path.

"Maybe I can help you there too," he said. "Find you a job."

She was surprised of course, thinking to herself, If the mayor starts finding jobs for every person who walks into his office...

"Well, sure, if you hear of something."

But Le Bars wasn't interested in his own answer anymore, only in the time it gave him to move closer to the sofa where she was sitting, her legs still squeezed together, with even her knees wishing they could escape the repeated glances he couldn't help giving them. On the last syllable of her sentence, he pulled what seemed like a magic trick: He came over to the slightly anachronistic leather sofa and sat down, not facing her, but next to her, at a distance you wouldn't call intimate, because of the five or six inches he had yet to conquer, or maybe he wouldn't need to, figuring that he'd already done the hardest part, the fact that when he came closer she hadn't jumped to her feet, much less tried to leave in the seconds that followed. He could now continue the conversation as if nothing had changed, as if it were perfectly normal for a mayor and a girl to be sharing a sofa during an ordinary first meeting.

"You need to give me your contact information so I can reach you in case..."

Laura looked at him wide-eyed, taken aback or simply caught short, and said, "Yes, of course. But wouldn't it be simpler if you just told my father?"

Again, he felt like a draft was blowing between them, as though Max's ghost were insinuating itself into the big office and couldn't be allowed to stay, because the entire fragile edifice Le Bars was slowly erecting might collapse. The main obstacle, he sensed, was that at any moment Max could appear in the room, like a hologram, to create a kind of wall between them. And this was the very wall that Laura suddenly felt the need to raise, without realizing how much of it was a kind of natural, unconscious defense, provided it protected her from Le Bars, as if each time she said "my father," Max would appear in a corner of the room and she could go hide behind him, the way a shy child clings to a grown-up's leg.

"Yes," said Le Bars, "but it really would be simpler if you gave me a phone number, so I can pass your contact information on."

"Of course," she said.

"Do you have any special skills?"

"Beg pardon?"

"I don't know. Do you speak English? Have you already been working?"

"Yes, a little..." Feeling torn, she hesitated about telling the truth, then continued: "In a bar."

"Really, in a bar? Did you like it?"

"Sure."

But from that point on, he was no more interested in what he was saying than in her answers, each word serving only to fill the time that would allow him to take charge of the situation. It didn't take Laura long to understand—or at least for it to occur to some part of her awareness—that he had other ideas in mind, that with each slowly passing second, it was as if he had a seismograph in his pocket to measure the vibrations she gave off while he very gently approached what we'd have to call the epicenter, except that the earthquake hadn't happened yet. For the time being, plates were merely being invisibly subducted, floating on a kind of magma, driven solely by his desire. And then, while he was speaking, it happened, like the moment of impact occurs in plate tectonics: She felt him put his hand on hers, and say, "I'll do what I can to help you."

Laura felt her breath catch, like someone driving a nail into a clock to stop its hands from moving, and she didn't move for several long seconds, feeling dumbfounded, with her brain at a standstill, just suspended, not thinking or hesitating, with nervous energy making its way up to her brain, but getting stuck there, like an elevator stuck between two floors.

"I can't tell you how long it took me to take my hand from under his," she told the policemen. "I just remember that I did, and I slipped it into my free hand, and I stood up," not quickly enough, she would think later, that is, not in a way that would mean that it was nothing doing. At least that was what she figured in hindsight, but in hindsight only.

Embarrassed, or maybe annoyed, Le Bars ended the meeting while offering a bridge to the future. He stood up in turn and said, "All right, I'll see what I can do for you." Stepping over to his desk, he took a pen and a small notebook and asked her to write her phone number in it. "That was his thing too," she told the policemen. "A way of suggesting that he wasn't treating me like just anybody," that he was putting her number in a personal notebook. There are people like that, she said, "who can make you feel you're the only person in the world."

Le Bars then held out his business card with his name printed next to the city's coat of arms. He just held it out, without giving it to her. She would clearly remember the moment when the card was between their two hands, as if suspended in midair above a precipice. He continued holding it lightly, and she could feel the paper bridge connecting them and didn't dare pull harder to take it. Then he said, "If you need anything at all, don't hesitate to call me." Finally, he let go. She thanked him again, holding the card without knowing where to put it. Accustomed to wrapping up meetings like this, he walked her to the door, his hand on the small of her back to propel her toward the exit, repeating one last time that he would look into her situation.

5

He would call her all right, Le Bars thought; no doubt about that. The only question was to know when. Behind his big office windows, Le Bars could be seen watching Laura as she disappeared under the stone portico. Having checked the time, he put his phone to his ear and asked Max to come get him. Max had also seen her come out of city hall, his big girl in her wool dress. He was sitting at the wheel of the municipal limousine parked at the back of the courtyard, waiting to be called, like a taxi. He followed Laura with his eyes as she walked in the shadow of the brown stones. It was as if Max and the mayor were taking turns watching her, like passing a relay baton, two paired cameras whose overlapping fields of view covered her reality, or a television control room standing by to switch from one screen to another. Max didn't say hello to her or dare roll down his window, even as she walked the length of his car. In his rearview mirror, he watched her tall figure quickly walking away. Laura was too worried to even see him, too busy replaying the film of the meeting in her mind. He also didn't say hello because his phone rang just as she was passing like a shadow in front of him. It was Le Bars. Max immediately started the car and pulled up at the foot of the stairs. He got out and opened the back door as Le Bars said, "To the Neptune, Max, I'm running late." He got back behind the wheel, accelerated briskly as usual, and drove through the narrow gateway leading outside the city walls. To the mayor he then said, "It's high tide today, we'll have to go around."

That's the way it is in this city. On days when the tide is high, the sea lies at exactly the same level as the town stretching behind it, to the point that from the road you would think you could touch it in calm weather, as if it were pavement and you could walk on it like an esplanade. But if by any chance the offshore wind and swell join forces to drive the ocean more strongly inland, the waterfront road is closed, submerged by breaking waves. On those days, you have to detour through back streets to get out of the old city, which stands like a granite island on the verge of sinking.

The mayor and his driver talked about the increasingly violent high tides, and what this said about climate change, that at this rate it would be like Venice, a city of canals and peeling walls. "Instead of a car, I'll need an inflatable Zodiac to drive you around," Max told the mayor. Jumping into the silence that followed, he asked if it had gone well with Laura. Le Bars was expecting the question, the way a batter expects the ball as it is thrown. He pretended to be lost in thought, then seemed to come back to reality, as if he were waking up. "What?" he said.

"Oh, yes, it went very well. We'll see what we can do for her."

"Will you find her an apartment?"

"I'll try," he said.

Max was already slowing as he approached the Neptune, where a valet stood in the distance, ready to rush to the door to greet the mayor and escort him into the great hall with its panoramic view of the sea. Le Bars regularly met various bankers, promoters, or political figures there, because that's the way it was at the Neptune. The city's notables and councillors would bump into each other often, pretending when they met that mere fate had brought them together. If one of those fortuitous encounters led to a lucrative opportunity, well, it was because that same fate had arranged things, like a thick smoke designed to hide calculation or collusion, in the same way that Romans used to meet in the baths. The Neptune was so deeply anchored in the city's mores that the mayor himself couldn't have done without it even if he'd wanted to. Certainly not Mayor Le Bars, who was like a fish in water there, happily encountering other fishes of the same species, one of whom was waiting at a table. His name was Franck Bellec, and he was wearing a white suit.

There aren't fifty people in the whole city with a white suit. You have priests on Sunday as the churches let out, maybe a few wedding couples at city hall on Saturday, and then you have Franck Bellec, the casino manager and a close friend of the mayor, who handed his jacket to the waiter and sat down at the table. Glancing around the hall to make sure no one could hear him, Le Bars waved to a few people sitting a little farther away, then almost whispered, "You'll never guess who just left my office."

"Who?" asked Bellec.

"Max Le Corre's daughter."

Bellec had been lounging at his ease and looking out at the sea, which almost reached the bottom of the picture windows. On hearing the name Max Le Corre, he jerked back in his chair and swallowed hard.

For Bellec, that name wasn't just some line in the civil register, as Le Bars knew perfectly well, more like an entry in an old book of spells that had been yanked open, sending the dust of another, forgotten time drifting through the air.

"Max's daughter?" asked Bellec.

"Yes," said the mayor. "I think you know her."

"I thought she was in Rennes."

"That's right. She was, but she's come back to be with her father. He sent her to me. He'd like me to find an apartment for her."

Each time Le Bars said Max's name, Franck's heart gave a lurch so hard it wouldn't take a stethoscope to detect it, but he maintained that look of indifference he knew how to feign, forcing himself to go on eating as if they were chatting about the weather.

"So what do you plan to do?"

"I don't know," said Le Bars. "I can't just wave a magic wand and produce an apartment."

Franck was absentmindedly saying "Yes" and "For sure," while thinking, Why are you telling me this? It doesn't concern me, and more to the point, I don't *want* it to concern me.

Then Le Bars added, "We might be able to help her in the meantime."

His fork paused in its movement toward his mouth, and Franck looked up from his plate and said, "What do you mean 'we'?"

But there was no need for the mayor to say anything more, because Franck understood enough to quickly grasp the situation. It was like he'd been examining the details of a large painting under his nose and then abruptly stepped back a few feet to see it as a whole. He could also see the mayor's request as a whole—along with his own complicity—because of the long-standing and complex relationship that connected them. This was a matter of common knowledge, despite everything that at first glance set them apart. The one, looking neat and proper in tailored suits that stretched over an expanding girth, the other inexorably connected with the dark side of the world. The whiteness of Franck's suit would never redeem him. If anything, it just further exposed him, the way at twilight a car's headlights remind you that night is falling.

"You could probably find something for her, Franck," the mayor continued.

"I... I'm not sure I'm the right person for that."

If anyone near them heard their conversation, they would be baffled by what followed, unable to grasp what was really being said behind words as abstract as "we" or "something." On the one hand, the two men seemed versed in a grammar of pronouns and ellipses, like two Mafiosi whose code of honor was to never call things by their names. On the other hand, they'd clearly had this kind of conversation before, if not the very same one, otherwise how could they understand each other while using such a limited vocabulary whose concrete facts seemed hidden in the corners of the language behind which the evidence of a shared reality was being deployed? Otherwise, how could Franck have answered, "I . . . I don't know. Usually the rooms are for the casino staff, not for . . ."

Franck glanced right and left in turn, afraid that he had spoken too loudly or too clearly. Le Bars seemed to be expecting his reluctance, partly because he knew him well and partly because in the car that brought him here, he'd had time to exactly preview the course of their discussion, like a chess game he had played before.

"That's what I told her, too," Le Bars promptly replied.

"What do you mean? What did you tell her?"

"That I would be able to help her find her a job."

"In my casino? Help her find her job in my casino?"

Le Bars didn't see any problem in getting work for a kid going through a tough patch, whereas for Franck, that problem was the *only* thing he saw. Le Bars is obviously dazzled by her, he thought, but this is out of the question. He can't do this. Still, he knew Le Bars, whose forbidding gaze under his heavy eyebrows hid all that capricious energy throbbing behind it, as stubborn as a child hopping from foot to foot, while he maintained the somewhat chilly dignity of a person who clearly had no problem with his conscience.

"It shouldn't be very hard for you, and besides..."

Because of the way Le Bars paused in mid-sentence, Franck didn't need to hear the rest, didn't need to hear everything that was being forcefully said with that single locution "and besides." Franck had silently understood and interpreted "and besides" not to be a trump card that the other man was about to put down on the table, merely a reminder that their two destinies were sufficiently linked that Franck wouldn't be able to disengage himself just like that. Everyone knew that Bellec's office was just a branch office of the mayoralty, a place where more important decisions were taken than in the city council, so much so that some had dubbed it the "ministry of finance," calling Bellec the city's great moneyman. In a way, that's what he was, a top-level treasurer, to the point that no mayor, banker, or local big shot failed to pay regular visits to the prince. That part was true. He was sometimes called the prince, and it was understood by all that the power in the city had two centers and two faces, the mayor's and Bellec's. With that "and besides" still ringing in Franck's ears, Le Bars was merely reminding him of what they were for each other: two spiders whose webs had been entangled for so long that you could never tell which spinneret had produced the thread that held them together, keeping them obligated to each other, as if they had knighted each other in a kind of twisted, bijective vassalhood that only people of power know how to maintain their whole lives, smilingly calling it by the beautiful name of friendship. Yes, it was all that, all that "friendship" suddenly encompassed in the expression "and besides," that Le Bars hardly needed to expand on it for Franck to understand that if someone ever took a broom to sweep the ceiling, the two spiders would fall down together and the whole town with them, as if hanging from a clothesline that one of the Fates could cut in a moment of anger.

And who could have suspected that this particular Fate would be a twenty-year-old girl with a name less mythical than Lachesis or Clotho, but who held in her hands the same sharp scissors that she now unwittingly threatened to close on the taut thread of their webs? In any event, Franck Bellec already perceived this as a distant threat, too distant and too disconnected from his own caprice for Le Bars to measure it, to the point that at the moment when the sentence "After all, you owe me this" would fall in Franck's brain, it wouldn't be a simple veil that would cloud his vision but an entire wall of stones that would come together into a black screen. In other words, the mayor had just let Bellec know, in franker terms and in a language less economical than usual, that if he refused, others not a mile away were eager to step up, waiting for him to back out.

"All right," he said, "we'll give it a try."

As he conceded the victory to Le Bars, Franck's gaze moved to the beams of sunlight shining on the carpet, and he suddenly lost himself in each mote of the dust that had been raised and was now gently swirling in the air like shards of quartz or mica he might have studied under a microscope. Amid all that luminous dust, something inside him told Franck that he had just turned his casino into a gigantic ammunition dump, in which Laura was the main powder keg and Max Le Corre the match just waiting to be struck.

6

ll stories have one thing in common: a barren past, a foundation that underpins everything else. In books, the story is told in the pluperfect. In some old paintings, it's a ruined landscape in the background. Max and Franck knew each other well, or rather had known each other well, but in small towns, where people suspect they will be living side by side until they die, age and mistrust teach you to keep the right distance from each other. After a thousand days spent as brothers, you're later able to greet each other politely, almost as if nothing had gone before. Looking at the person, you barely recall that you were once close, but every hug you exchange out of habit still suggests the path you have shared, like a cast shadow. Max and Franck's shared path stretched back miles, all the years when Bellec was nothing less than Le Corre's manager, and more than his manager: the man who launched his career and pushed it, not to say built it, to the point that Max often said that without Franck he would never have become the professional boxer that—to hear him tell it—he'd never wanted to be.

But the fact is that when you have a gift for something, you're forced to love it, especially if someone walks into a small-town gym, points you out, and dazzles you with a glimpse of an exciting future. Especially if that man is named Franck Bellec, whose white suit was already brightening the halls of the city. It had been a long time since those penniless nights when he was the only person who thought he had the manners of a prince as he prowled the slums, reaching for every hand, like an apprentice dealer who already knows he's going to seize power. That same white suit, so mocked and anachronistic, so judged by the most blinkered imaginations, was like a challenge that Franck raised in the night, a kind of inner contract intimately connected to what some call ambition, to the point that people thought it came down to that, to his shifting the suit's whiteness from being a laughingstock to commanding absolute respect.

In that sense, you could say that Max was the first stage of Bellec's rocket. When Franck saw him box, he felt he was holding the winning ticket in the national lottery. And if there's one thing you can't deny Franck, it's the intuition he had that day—and he'd be the first to admit surprise at how penetrating it was and how lucrative it would soon be—of glory years when you could see Max in the ring raising his arms even before the referee confirmed his victory, as his KO'd opponent struggled to get up from the mat, when the lights of the rings were brighter than day. But if Max was that shining sun, the one bathed in its rays and growing like a plant, faster than a tropical tree in a greenhouse, was Franck.

Even Marielle, Max's wife at the time, who didn't like Franck, or boxing, for that matter, soon realized this. As time passed, she saw the man she had married gradually get erased, and what difference did being married or not make? Instead of an adolescent with a hesitant gaze, she now endured Max the pugnacious boxer throwing himself body and soul into the madness of his sport. And never mind the body, she thought, but the soul was something else. Yes, the soul was something else, and Max seemed to have given it to Franck by a kind of metempsychosis, driven by the almost animal faith that Franck effortlessly worked to imbue him with. Over time, it was as if Franck had taken all the excess energy he couldn't expend himself and poured it into Max's body. Franck was on the short side, wiry and twitchy, but he radiated an unfocused brutality for which boxing seemed the first outlet and Max's body the first proxy. During bouts, you would see Franck in the front row, suffering even more than Max when he took punches, patting him on the back between rounds, and kissing him on the forehead when he won. Sometimes he even handed him the bouquet of flowers he'd been asked to deliver, while Max raised his arms to the tune of the winner's booming triumphant march, both men aware that the somewhat deafening brasses and percussion weren't the evening's end point but the opening credits of another, beckoning world, the endless world of the night. The city's big shots welcomed Max like a prodigal son, estates and seafront villas were suddenly open to him, along with swimming pools and evenings in his honor that raised him all the way up to his throne without his ever sensing that the others preferred their places to his—and Bellec most of all. From atavism or experience, they knew he was teetering atop stilts already gnawed by termites. Not one of them would have set foot on the rotten platform that served as his throne. They just let the champagne flow down from the top of the pyramid, happy to applaud the crowned man—Max when he was winning, say—as if he were the governor of an imaginary island, and the only person not to realize it.

That island, it should be said, was ruled by strange laws written in invisible ink, of the kind that in fairy tales are only glimpsed in old parchments and which few people can decipher, and certainly not Max, who happily stuck with the glossy paper of the magazines in which he sometimes appeared, caught by a photographer as the king of nocturnal glories. Except that among those immutable laws, one was written in bolder letters than the others in the great book of the night: that every king needs a queen. And that law, Max did not infringe. She even had a queen's name: Hélène. And she was Franck's sister.

They say that it was because of her that Max fell, that she had brought other men down, that she destroyed everything in her path. They say she was the deadliest of all the whores on the Breton coast, that she had a sixth sense for immediately grasping where the money was, or not the money—because everybody always knew that—but the flaw in the person who had it, as if her entire body were one big metal detector that could magnetize a man's heart and his fortune. How and on what day she entered Max's life has been lost in the sands of time, but she eventually fell into his arms like a grain of pollen drifting through the night in the glow of some nightclub, since that was Max's adopted exotic world and Hélène's native habitat, actually more bee than pollen, her gaze fertilizing all the flower-men sitting along the bars. Max wound up being one of them, in that upside-down world where pollen-gathering women eagerly slipped into the men's corollas and relieved them of all their stamens, only these stamens took the shape of hundred-euro bills that they spread around without counting, which seeds the women—less bees than wasps, which don't pollinate anything—scattered as one glass followed another, and Hélène was the most determined of them all, having imposed the tacit and inalienable law that this was her price and her liberty, the most expensive and freest of the hostesses.

Max, Hélène would one day tell Laura, was like a big ceramic piggy bank that boxing filled with gold coins and that people smashed into a thousand pieces in order to empty it. So she was there to glue the pieces back together, that is, give him the fake love that kept him profitable and strong enough to be stuffed with cash again, and smashed again, and so on. And either Max didn't notice what was going on or it suited him.

Of course if there was one person this did not suit, it was Marielle, who wasn't fooled by any of it. But by some trick of pride whereby we arrange things in our favor, she basically believed—out of love, or patience, or hope—that all this was just a fling, and for a long time went on believing that she dwelled in the heart of a truth that was more worthy and full of a future, the kind of future that Max fed with the promises they had made to each other, that boxing, they knew, would only last so long, that he would quit as soon as he could. As soon as he could meant when he had put enough money aside for the kind of future life that couples have a gift of inventing, provided they could find the illusion of what kept them together in it, but only the illusion, since in the meantime Max was sinking ever deeper into the royal night, so that with each promise he made to her, Marielle wound up seeing through a mirror without silvering that allowed her to observe her husband's untethered life, the sumptuous and, as it were, flourishing life being led by her bastard of a husband.

Was that the expression Marielle used in front of their thirteen-year-old daughter as she packed their suitcase and prepared to leave? In any case, Max was even less able to hear the final sentence she said just once on that October evening, exactly this: "I'm leaving, Max. I'm leaving you," before she disappeared into the foggy darkness, the door hardly slammed but closed enough for him to understand there was no returning. Neither for her, nor for Laura. And Max hadn't seen a thing coming. He thought he would still be wearing his royal crown for the next thousand nights, so it was like the carriage in the fairy tale suddenly turning back into a pumpkin, except that nobody had actually told Max there would be a midnight.

That midnight would last for some years—another thing he hadn't been warned about—as he took his endless fall, drifting away from the boxing rings without anyone trying to bring him back, not even Franck Bellec, least of all Franck Bellec, whom a recently elected Le Bars had asked to manage the casino. So that was how the white rocket jettisoned Max, its now useless first stage, into space, like metal shards exploding in a night whose glow was no longer the lighting of swimming pools in villa estates but the neon lights of bars at closing time, the yellowish tinge you wind up seeing in the bathroom mirror, with an urge to smash your own reflection with your bare hands.

7

mong the first things Franck told Laura was this: that he never would have expected to see Max boxing again. "No, not your father. It sure brings back memories. You know, your father and I were very close," he added, as if he felt the need to justify himself, with her sitting there, in an office only slightly more modest than the mayor's, though in a different style, with its bay window and big aquarium, its polished bookcases holding souvenirs from times past: There, in a lighted glass case and balanced like roses in a vase, were a pair of boxing gloves. The inscription on the metal stand read, "MAX LE CORRE, CHAMPION OF FRANCE 2002," like a holy relic that no later quarrel could spoil, as permanent as the centenary coat of arms displayed at the city gates. Max himself probably hadn't passed through Franck's office doors more than once or twice, but he could be sure that those gloves hadn't budged, that they remained Franck's great pride as well as his own. And as Franck watched Laura gazing at them, perhaps surprised to find them there, he tacitly thanked himself for contributing to this, too proud to underline it by saying, "You know, it was thanks to me that your father . . ." but even prouder of being able to leave it unsaid, reigning so high over the city that he didn't care if she knew. Because if there was one thing he suspected Max had never told his daughter, it was this: That without him, Max would never have been the boxer he was.

Franck went on to say that he also never would have expected to see Laura back in her hometown, that the last time he had seen her she was so small, ten or twelve maybe, and already very pretty, he couldn't help telling her, as she sat there, at his invitation, next to the round window that held all of the sea. He didn't dare ask for news of Marielle, though he could have: She would have answered that it was a very old story, and more walled off than the old city, adding that as the years went by, Marielle still didn't like Franck and had no desire to see him, or Max either, whom she met as often as she did only so he could see his daughter growing up.

But Franck didn't ask anything, didn't question Laura about what had brought her back, much less comment sarcastically about the advertising billboards where of course he had recognized her, and heard the anonymous muttering that ran through the streets like the wind, that yes, the erotic bombshell posing in her underwear on the bus stops was Max Le Corre's daughter. And he certainly didn't tell Laura that at the bottom of a desk drawer he had saved the magazine whose centerfold pages she had once graced, pages where underwear was no longer involved.

With the unfocused gaze of a child, Laura ran her eyes along the walls and the sea through the bay window reflected in the big glass case dominated by boxing gloves, next to photographs of all those who at one time or another thought it worth stopping by this local chancellery to pose with Franck in the place's dubious glory. On some of them, she even came across the face of her father in his platinum shorts with some minister or president from early in the century. He was still young, smiling with his hair dyed blond the way it was when he was twenty. Franck was always standing next to them, his white suit catching the eye like a charm, though you couldn't tell if it was a lucky one or not. The suit's repeated presence in each photograph seemed to concentrate the destiny of all those people smiling in the artificial night. Maybe because Franck himself in the flesh was right in front of her, Laura had the feeling that he'd pulled it off, that he'd managed to drag each person down to the irony of his passage on Earth, alabaster pale in his white suit and looking almost dead already, like those skulls set on a desk in the corner of a Baroque painting that underscore the vanity of all the objects in the canvas. Seeing the images again through the prism of Laura's gaze, Franck may have felt a bit sentimental, yielding for a moment to nostalgia for Max and for their friendship.

That's all very well, he thought, but that's not why she's here. He had Laura sit down on the leather chair opposite, and said, "Do you know that you come to me highly recommended?"

She tried to smile, without knowing whether it was from embarrassment or complicity.

"The mayor says you're looking for work."

"Yes. Well, no. Housing. I went to see him about an apartment. Well, it was my father who—"

"Oh, so you're not looking for a job?"

"Yeah, that too, but—"

"Because here the rule is, I only provide housing for the women who work."

"The women who work?"

"Yes, the girls who—"

"You mean the bar girls."

Franck was momentarily surprised, even taken aback. Then he told himself, this is Max's daughter, all right, with that same mix of weakness and pride, of sudden arrogance that comes across like a spasm of self-respect in the heart of servility. Those were the sort of things he thought, maybe in less elaborate form, but dark, condescending things, feeling strongly that Laura was talking to show that she was no fool, but in life not being a fool is never ever enough to keep you from giving in, he thought, and not giving in is something else, it calls for different strength, a different nature. You're acting clever, poor girl, but the fact is you're here. Without batting an eyelash, he continued: "We usually say hostess, but if you prefer, bar girl works too."

"You can't overcome harshness when it's acknowledged," said Laura later. "The only way out for me would have been to run away, but oddly enough, it doesn't do that. Instead, it acts like an electric shock you might give a dog to keep it from coming back. That's what it did to me," she said. "Crazy isn't it? It didn't make me angry, it made me obedient."

"I can make an exception for you," said Franck.

"Meaning what?"

"You wouldn't have to work."

Because of the density of Laura's gaze at that moment, Franck thought she was going to get up and leave, that she had no intention of being an exception, much less an object of pity for her father's sake, or worse, just as a favor. But that's not what she did. Instead, she said, "I need money."

"I understand. But I don't know if—" Franck interrupted himself because of what he didn't want to say. "You could work behind the bar. You wouldn't have to..." Concluding quickly, he said, "Anyway, it'll be temporary, until Quentin finds you proper housing."

"Quentin?"

"The mayor. His name is Quentin."

Not only was the mayor far from Laura's mind but she realized that she didn't know his first name, or that in any case she'd never separated it from his last one, so hearing "Quentin" by itself was like finding herself thrust too quickly into an unwanted intimacy.

"And where your father's concerned," Franck continued, "You can just tell him that..."

But he wasn't able to complete that sentence either, as if in that kind of lapse he had revealed the one thing that had been bothering him ever since Laura walked in. It was like an old pain he thought he'd been cured of that suddenly flared up again, like a piece of metal left in a body by a surgeon after an operation that long afterward starts to rust and affects the organs. It was doing this to Franck, with Laura now sitting there, having pierced the security perimeter he thought he had built between himself and Max, which that idiot Le Bars had now trampled against his will.

"I tell my father whatever I like," she said. "It's none of his business."

To Franck, sensing the wall standing so clearly between father and daughter, this felt like a liberation.

"I'll introduce you to Hélène," he continued. "She's in charge of the hall." Standing up to invite her to follow, he added, with the look of complicity that came so easily to him, "She's my sister."

Side by side, the two of them went downstairs one floor to the main gambling hall. Even at that time of day it was already full, though no daylight could be seen through the black curtains lining the whole room, or on the steel counter that marked off the bar and reflected the lights hanging from the high ceiling. Their filtered, somewhat mauve light said nighttime, or at least suggested it, even in broad daylight, if you were willing to forget the march of time. Perched on her tall stool, Hélène certainly wasn't there to set time right. Diminished by the years but still Franck's sister, set near the bar like a worn mascot, Hélène had suffered that accelerated aging that hits night people like a poleax. At thirty-five, she looked ten years older. Time had turned into a punishing god who decided to collapse her cheeks and swell her eyelids with all the excess alcohol her blood couldn't absorb.

"Hélène, this is Laura," Franck said. "She'll be working with us." Then, trying to pass off the matter as a mere detail, he added, "She's Max's daughter."

Luckily for him, Laura had already stuck out her hand, forcing Hélène to maintain the calm expression that masked her astonishment as they were being introduced. Certainly, something deep inside her suddenly twisted, a bitter pang in the pit of her stomach, but nothing showed on her face, with its bags and shadows, giving the impression that the women didn't know each other. And in a sense that was true, given that Laura had never heard Hélène spoken of. Her name had never passed her mother's lips, nor had any mention of a princely whore who had destroyed their marriage. Mareille stuck to more laconic, succinct formulations like "You're old enough to understand that my getting involved with Max was a youthful mistake." For his part, after his long fall through the night without boxing, Max never spoke to Hélène again. He would run into her at street corners, of course, but remained locked in a mute, paranoid funk, having broken with her world, of which he had so stupidly thought himself the undisputed king.

Hélène didn't push the lie so far as to smile at Laura, instead saving her somewhat unnerving reserve for the look she shot her brother, as if to say, more or less, You don't really expect Max's daughter to work here, do you? You don't expect her to whore for you? Franck could read every word written in his sister's dark eyes, and tried in turn to write the answer in his own, to make her understand that he didn't have a choice, that it was coming from higher up and would be very temporary. But whether Hélène read her brother's eyes or not, she got down off her stool and said to Laura, "I'm busy, we'll talk later."

Laura watched her walk away in the high heels she never shed, almost hypnotized by her self-confident stride. Then she caught herself and asked Franck, "So what about the room?"

"Ah, that's right, the room," he said. He too had been taken by his sister's figure as she walked away, just as he would've seized any pretext to suspend time and not have to act, especially not to launch the mechanism he knew was almost irreversible, before giving in and taking Laura to the room all the way upstairs.

She followed Franck to the stairs that led up under the roof, the long hallway with numbered doors, former storerooms long since remodeled into bedrooms, or, better than bedrooms, more like studio apartments with a big Velux skylight that flooded them with light. Standing on tiptoe, Laura could see the sea and the tall black rocks that no high tide ever covered. She walked around the room, trying to thank him. Propped in the doorway she saw reflected in the big wall mirror, Franck said, "I'm not the person you should thank, you know. It's the mayor."

With an expression that was hard to read, a look that suggested he would rather not go on but had to, Franck added, "He told me he would stop by to see that you're settled in."

Then the sea, which Laura had been gazing at so lightly a moment before, suddenly seemed to pull very far back, the way it's said to do before a tidal wave returns to sweep in a single crest over the tops of buildings. In the only way she had to show her surprise, she asked, "Who?"

Even Franck found it painful to repeat the name, though he said it several times a day, painful to imagine the man coming in here, knowing more or less what would happen next. In the end, he said it anyway: "Le Bars."

"How so? Stop by where?"

But Bellec was already heading off down the corridor, moving on to something else, saying, "I'll let you settle in. Go see Hélène about the hall." He was still moving away, acting as if she understood Le Bars's visit as well as he did, given what it had already cost him to mention it. Franck figured it wasn't up to him to prepare her for what no one could ever know. Sensing that she was sincerely surprised, maybe he felt an inner twinge, suddenly realizing that she was more naïve or younger than he thought, but what difference did that make? Nothing that justified his interfering between two grown, responsible adults, he told himself. It was none of his business. Besides, Franck had long since isolated what little heart he still had, the way you might isolate an instrument in a soundproof room.

8

t wouldn't have changed anything if Franck had warned her. In some parts of the brain, the gears don't mesh that quickly. So when Laura opened the door and saw Quentin Le Bars, half smiling, he looked like a photo cut out of a magazine that had been pasted there in the shadow of the threshold. He greeted her without the least embarrassment, and waited for her to ask him in, the way she might for a gas company employee who had come to read the meter, except that with his white shirt stretched over the curve of his belly, and without the necktie he must have just stuffed in his pocket, he didn't look like a gas company employee.

"As you see," he said, "I kept my word."

And then Laura, age twenty, a student, smiled at the forty-eight-year-old mayor of the city the way she'd been taught, and stepped back to let him in, and he, without hesitation kissed her on both cheeks. In his eyes, she could read the mix of... No, that was later, she said. It was only later that she was able to discern the somewhat worried look he carried like an unfinished childhood, the heavy, slightly raised eyebrows that might lead you to believe that he had some goodwill, or concern for the world, or... But no, there was none of that, only the fact that even the devil doesn't always wear a red suit and have flames in his eyes.

He was already walking around the room, as if he needed to get used to the place or suspected there was a microphone hidden somewhere, or was wondering if he could live in a place like this. Laura thought that when people entered some new place, whether a castle or a shack, they all wondered if could live there. "At least that's the way I am," she told the policemen. "In my dreams I'm able live in any house in the world, but maybe I've got a problem with living someplace."

In the room, Le Bars didn't need to stand on tiptoe to look out through the big skylight framing the horizon and the gray sky as far as the ramparts jutting out into the sea, all of which he was seeing as if this were a foreign city, as a visitor who would soon be returning to his far-off country. Then, very quietly and carefully, he said, "You're well set up here."

She nodded yes without daring to say the word, while he turned away from the light and walked around the room like a prowler looking for a place to scale a wall, stopping, hesitating a moment, then abruptly sitting down on the edge of the bed.

"It was only then that I realized that there was nowhere else to sit in the room except the bed," she said. Nowhere else to maintain the distance that might have spared her all the rest, but there, unless she sharply said no, unless she made him look ridiculous sitting there, that distance wasn't possible, she had to melt like snow in the sun.

"I was still standing up, you understand," she said. "It was as if I had made him feel uncomfortable, or I didn't have any manners, see, and he must have felt it, because right away he said, 'Aren't you going to sit down?'"

To the police officers she swore she didn't sit down right away, one eye on the big mirror reflecting her awkwardness back at her, another gazing inside herself, trying to figure what was happening, because in that instant, and only in that instant, in the few seconds when she hesitated to sit down, did she understand that she was about to make a decision, like signing the bottom of a contract that would be hard to break and all of whose clauses she had already accepted and had initialed the endorsements, which hadn't been written yet but whose every movement she felt represented entire pages dense with written obligations.

"All I can tell you," she continued, "is that what oppresses us sometimes isn't the panic of the moment but getting a sudden look at our own future."

The two policemen glanced at each other, increasingly wondering who it was they were dealing with, given the somewhat digressive and disaffected way she had of telling her story, as if it didn't really belong to her but she was watching herself tell it, without ever trying to appeal to their feelings. They eventually figured this was just her way of getting there.

"But actually, I had already signed that contract."

"How so?" asked one cop.

"I mean, that's the image I had at that moment, the image of all those pages I was holding in my hand and it was too late to tear them up in front of him, too late to ask him to leave now, him, the mayor of the city. No, I'm telling you, it was signed."

And then yes, she sat down on the edge of the bed next to him, not too close, but still. And in the silence that fell between them, under the signature she had just put there on the last page, it was as if a huge forest suddenly grew up, made of a thousand tiny signs they were both trying to decipher at the speed of light—he, her availability (he could have thought: her fragility; but no, he thought: her availability), she, his desire (she could have thought: his vulgarity; but no, she thought: his desire)—and then very slowly, without saying another word, he took her hand in his.

"That was the exact moment when it really happened, not the next one, not later," she said. "Not even when I had his cock in my hand." Yes, she said it that crudely, whereas up to then she'd been so reluctant to give the facts in their simplicity, that is to say their brutality, and suddenly it popped out like that, without the slightest detour, a simple story of organs that shouldn't have met, and because maybe it would have been worse for her not to say it that way, to persist with all the silences and the circumlocutions that had let the image float in her for some time, and to say what? A thing that could fit in the simplest statement in the world—his cock, therefore, in her hand.

"Yes," she continued, "when I felt the warm palm of his hand, it was as if my hand wasn't mine anymore, that he had managed to seize, or control, or, I don't know, magnetize all the living energy in me. In any case he took power then, and when I lifted my hand, when he moved it very gently toward his belt, to the contrary, if I can explain it, to the contrary from then on it was as if the world was slowly reshaping itself, I mean as if everything that followed, every gesture and word that followed, wasn't there to increase the blast of the explosion but actually to ensure that all this was logical, that it was all coherent, and as if ordered by some god I didn't recognize but who seemed to know what he was doing. In any case I gave myself over to this unknown god, for everything that would happen in that room on that day."

Le Bars took the time that was necessary, maybe counting the seconds, the way that before surgery the anesthesiologist waits for the injection to work, seeing if the dose of curare or, I don't know, some extra-powerful drug, was the right dose for the right body, that is, to see whether she was going to shout, or leap to her feet, or slap him. "But as for me, I didn't move," she said. "I mean, no more than he would have wanted me to move at that moment, just my hand, which was moving like an inanimate object toward him, that is, toward the shape of his cock, which was already stiff."

At that point, she let a long silence spool out that the two cops didn't dare break, as if she were considering the order of things and was having trouble setting it straight.

"He said he could help me," she continued. "I did it because he said that first: 'I want to help you, Laura.'"

"Are you sure he put his hand on yours?"

She closed her eyes a little by way of acquiescence.

"But after that?"

"After that, I don't know. His look, maybe. Or a slight tug on my hand, or else I just thought that..." She again fell silent, looking at the floor.

"That what?"

"Then that was the way it happens."

"What do you mean?" asked one cop. "What happens that way?"

"I don't know. That sort of thing. That of course if you've gotten to that point, on the edge of a big bed in a room with a man like that, well, there you go, yeah, you do it."

"You do it?"

"Yeah, you do it, that is you let his hand guide you to his cock, and you understand that it's up to you to undertake..." That was the word she used, "undertake." That she was the one who undertook it.

"He didn't ask you for anything?"

"No. Not really."

"So you did it of your own free will?"

"No, I'm telling you, it was what I was supposed to do. That doesn't mean that it was my free will."

The two cops began to get annoyed.

"Wait, you said he didn't ask you for anything," one insisted.

"No, nothing. In any case he didn't say, 'Get undressed' or 'Lie down.' No, he didn't say anything like that." And for a simple reason, which she had since understood: He needed to lie to himself, that is, something in him needed to leave that room with the feeling that it had nothing to do with him, that he wasn't the one who had acted, but that it was her, that only his body had yielded and no part of his will, that yes, he was surprised to find her hand on his cock, surprised to tilt his head back slightly, that suddenly he wasn't himself, but as if enchanted by this slut who just wanted to suck his cock, and he, what had he done beyond yielding to the fundamental laws of nature? What had he done beyond doing her a favor, as she sought the warmth of his cock? Those were all the thoughts he marshaled for a long time, the kind of thoughts he would need to help himself overcome the bitterness of his vice, unless, no: These were the kind of thoughts that *she*, Laura, would need to have to imagine him as bitter, or guilty, or simply sad in order to tolerate her own bitterness or sadness when he stood up so quickly ten minutes later, got dressed so fast, and vanished so quickly into the night, barely looking back as he closed the door.

9

"Didn't it occur to you to file a complaint then?" asked one of the policemen.

"Occur to me? Yeah, maybe, but the idea must have zipped by like a comet in the dark, because I don't remember it. On that day, it was more like I was filing a complaint against myself, so to speak."

And in a way that's what Laura was doing an hour later, stretched out on the beach, unsure whether to close her eyes or let the damp wind fill them, with the gradually rising tide that would soon embrace her, with that thing that was so strange, so intimate and undesirable, that seemed to accompany her, the shame, maybe, that kept rustling inside her, and neither the rocks nor the calm water could still the murmuring between her temples and leave it there, like an abandoned weapon at the foot of the ramparts, fairly covered with seaweed and wrack, or that a breeze might carry away on the surface of the water, but no, that didn't happen. She saw nothing of the strollers on the beach or the rocks at low tide, and little of the dogs running by the water's edge or the stooped seashell collectors, no, she didn't see anything of the peaceful life that manages to keep going alongside misfortune—or not misfortune but stupor—hoping that if she smoked and smoked some more she would get rid of the too salty, too acrid smell of her sweat. Lying under the hazy late-afternoon sun, she had to stand up to feel the wind that was still fresh, and then what? Look at the horizon to remember that there was one, though it seemed that no brightness was enough to widen it. That's how she felt afterward, as soon as she left the room, in fact, and ran downstairs to get outside for some air then started walking and walking all over the old city and on the rocks, and then she lay down here, like a beached whale that the water would soon cover, hoping to be able to head for the open ocean someday, hoping that the tide would soon lift her clangorous soul and she would again be free to roam the world's seas. But for now, the only thing that seemed to be rising from the seafloor were all the sea goddesses appearing in the whispering spray, who had decided to speak to her, or rather declaim, as they did so well when commenting on the action. And it was like having the leader of an antique chorus in the corner of the evening, an assembly of fifty naiads around her, chanting, "Oh, Laura, what have you done? What have you done?"

Eventually, she had to leave the beach as night fell. Had to go back upstairs to that room where she opened the skylight to air out the room, the smell, and the meaning of her actions. Had to wash herself, spending a long time under very hot water. From her purse, had to take the antianxiety pills she carried everywhere and which she used to gulp by the handful during her modeling days. And the water, the drugs, the sleep almost worked. She woke up the next day and everything seemed far away. She even told herself, That's that, it's over, we're even.

"Yeah, that's what I thought," she continued in front of the policemen. "That now it was finished, now I was in my own place, and it was finished. I thought that, I swear."

"Meaning what? You believed that?"

"I think there are some things I'm not sure you can understand," she said.

"No?"

In the silence that she allowed to settle, she wondered how she could explain it to them, how to tell them that the second step is much higher than the first.

And in fact it was true, they didn't seem to understand, any more than if you had put a mathematical equation reduced to its most abstract expression in front of them, like they were high schoolers, willing enough, but whose turn of mind wasn't suited to those kinds of metaphors, unable to come up with anything more than a kind of literal image of a staircase with uneven steps.

"The hardest thing," she continued, "or the worst, or the most absurd, isn't going from zero to one, but going from one to two, you understand, meaning going from the first time to the second time."

"You mean there was a second time?"

"The next day. At the same time. They came to get me at the bar and said, 'He's waiting.'"

"Who was this 'they'?"

"I don't know. Someone."

"And you went?"

"Yes."

At this, the cop who was typing her account on the computer stopped, as if he couldn't go on recording a complaint that he considered more and more pointless.

"I don't understand," he said. "You certainly could have said no at that point."

"Maybe," she said. "I don't know." And she continued, almost irritated or else still thinking aloud, "Do you know why the second time is worse than the first? Because that time, the second time, contains all the following ones."

And the other cop, the calmer one, who was afraid of breaking something in the now smooth unfolding of her account, said in a quieter tone, "Yes, of course I understand."

"No, I don't think so," she told him. "I don't think you really understand, because it's not possible, it's just not possible, because then you would know more than I do, and that doesn't make any sense." As she said that last word, she set her elbows on the desk, as if wanting to put an exclamation point at the end of her sentence, of a kind that no language could really translate.

"Maybe it's your job to gather the facts," she continued, "even to make them fit together like a house of cards, but I'm telling you that all I have to do is walk over and just breathe on it, and I'll make your house of cards collapse. And you know why? Because it's my house, with my cards."

10

She said she could remember every single time in the tiniest detail, could describe the color of the sky and the few minutes he was on top of her, or she was on top of him, or... It never lasted long, she said, because of that way all politicians had of showing up in the middle of the day between two meetings, wanting nothing more than to satisfy that sick, urgent male desire as quickly as possible. She also said that after a while she forgot that she had drifted into this situation against her will, as if she wasn't able to stay absent from her own body so often, almost forgetting that she was doing it to get something, an apartment. She didn't dare mention that again, but as the days went on, she understood that it would never happen, unless she was silently clinging to it to justify her behavior in her own eyes, but that was probably one of the most subtle workings of the machinery, that as the days passed, it managed to make their relationship seem necessary even though it fell short of her goal, fell short of the straightforward deal they seemed to have tacitly struck, like a tribal pact where the trade object itself gets forgotten in the mechanical and ritual character of the exchange.

She would expect him every evening, or almost, around five o'clock, her only client, in a way. She would be sitting on a stool at the casino bar, with Bellec stationed at the other end of the counter looking at Hélène as if asking for her permission, and then coming over to Laura to let her know that the mayor had just arrived and was waiting for her upstairs. She would excuse herself to the customers, quickly down the flute of champagne someone had bought her, and say, "I'll be back." And Franck, not daring to look at Hélène, would follow her with his eyes to the dimly lit stairs she started to climb. Showing her annoyance, Hélène would slam her glass down on the steel counter, and often ostentatiously get up to go stand by the window, pulling the always drawn curtains aside. Looking outside was her way of showing her disapproval, forcing her brother to remember that down below, in a black limousine with tinted windows, an old boxer was waiting who had no idea of what was going on. And she would stand there for long seconds, staring, wondering how this could be happening.

It should be said that anyone could walk from city hall to the casino ten times a day, but not Le Bars, who always went by car, and not even Max knew whether it was out of sheer laziness or discretion—or cynicism, he might have added, if he'd only known. And if there is one itinerary whose every inch of asphalt Max knew, it was that one, leading from the city hall courtyard to the rear of the casino, past the historic galleons moored with their bows pointing at the ramparts, then slipping out of view into the parking lot, stopping not in front of the red-carpeted steps that made the clients feel important but at the small back door to the service stairs through which Le Bars had been visiting Franck for years. Le Bars asked Max to drop him off. Over the slamming of the door, he said, "Wait for me here, I won't be long."

But what could the driver have known, sitting in his car at the foot of the building, using the break to tilt his seat back a little and turn up the car radio volume, glad to finally be alone to read his boxing magazine while humming along with the pop tune on the radio? Just imagine him, Max Le Corre, his fingers tapping on the steering wheel, letting himself be borne along by some American singer's tune, while a few yards above him another man, the mayor, was also being borne along, but in his own way, with unseeing eyes—a montage that you could do in a film, alternating between Max's voice belting out the song's chorus, and Laura's head, which the mayor was pressing harder against his belly so he could feel the back of her throat with his cock, as if the father was singing at the top of his lungs, using his voice to drown out something he had no reason to know, which he shouldn't know, which he should never know. They say that it's terrible for children to imagine their parents having sex, but maybe it's even worse for a father to imagine his daughter who...

But that wasn't the case. Max wasn't imagining anything. He was singing, or dozing over the magazine that was sure to have an article about his opponent in their upcoming fight, who was already training at the gym he would go to in an hour, unaware of the additional rage he would be able to summon as he pounded the heavy punching bag.

Hélène's gaze encompassed all this as she looked from the first-floor windows, telling herself that it couldn't be happening, all the irony that was making the car even blacker, and the man she had known well so naïve. In her mind, she could see Laura's face harden when Franck came to whisper in her ear, then see her again fifteen minutes later, taking the last steps down to the gambling hall's thick carpet. Hélène even noticed that as the days passed, Laura did it better and better, because of her ability to believe that she had mastered the situation, having placed her pride right at that particular place, convincing herself while coming down the stairs and returning to the hall under the eyes of the women—who all knew where she'd been—that her strength stemmed from the level gaze she managed to maintain, maybe the way a stuntman bailing out of a flaming car keeps his cool, knowing he's being watched.

But the day had to come when Hélène, in the kind of montage of looks she projected on the father one moment and on the daughter the next, couldn't take it anymore: Seeing Max open the rear door, seeing him bow and scrape, she may have told herself that it just couldn't go on. And maybe it was this day more than another because she overheard their conversation in the parking lot. Le Bars looked at the seagull droppings on a rear fender and said, "Hey, Max, the car's very dirty, you ought to get it washed."

"You're right," said Max. "I'll take care of it."

Yes, that was the moment Hélène told herself that this couldn't go on. Releasing the partly opened curtain she'd been holding, she moved out of the light from the bar. The mayor had only just slipped into the building when she went downstairs and out to the parking lot, her high heels striking the ground, eroticizing the air just by walking through it. Max didn't see her coming, but when she walked around the front of the car and along the bumper right under his eyes, he couldn't not notice her as she approached and was soon standing by the driver's-side window.

To Max, seeing her so close felt weird, after all those years when he had avoided or ignored her, sometimes glimpsing her from afar but maintaining that maximum distance he needed in order to flee his own demons, and now here she was, leaning toward him, her elbows almost on the car door, her breasts pushed up and her breath full of the liquor she'd been drinking. Having Hélène suddenly so close, Max didn't think she was faded or bruised; instead he felt as if time had collapsed, and her two faces, the old and the new, were merging, allowing him to recapture the memory of her youth, when her glamour shone across the whole casino stage onto Max's skin and Franck's white suit.

He was tempted to tell her to fuck off, that he had nothing to say to her, that sort of thing, but all those years had diluted his anger, so he just sat there, facing forward so as not to meet her eye, trying to dredge up a rage that now escaped him. She was no longer the evil queen who had dragged him to the depths of the night, but a poor woman who had approached his car waving a white flag, he felt, almost a sister in sorrow. So when she said, "Hi, Max, it's been a long time," with that heavy smoker's voice that had gone almost hoarse in only five years, he turned his head toward her and muttered, "Hello," aware that with that single word, in its merely phatic function, he was settling many accounts, and in a sense almost reconciling himself with himself. And it was true: As long as he stayed wrapped in the blackness of days past, as long as he wasn't able to repaint that room in his memory, something that had been bothering him suddenly got unkinked by greeting Hélène through the car window, and not only her but a whole chunk of his own history, without yet realizing that certain pieces of memory are best not reopened, not even to air them out, thinking you're getting rid of the dust. To the contrary, it's best to keep them locked up, and keep them that way your whole life. But now, having opened the lock, he found everything intact in the reopened room, starting with the love potion that had intoxicated him a thousand times and whose charm, he realized, still worked.

And it was as if they had both opened the same lock at the same time, that just by looking into each other's eyes they had used the same crowbar to force open the same door, and a rush of desire silently seized them. A few hours later, they were lying on a bed, magically transported back years, aware of both the artifice and the cottony joy of experiencing such a state again, like two figurines in a snow globe being shaken, yes, they had the right to that for a while, to the entire reminiscence of their boozy story behind the drawn curtains of her room.

Hélène lay on her back, eyes fixed on the ceiling, and lit a cigarette. As ardor and desire slowly faded in the warmness of the sheets, she remembered that she hadn't gone to Max for this, not just to revive those nostalgic hours. In any case, that's when she recalled the image of Laura getting off her stool and apologizing to the customers, of Franck nodding to her, having said something like, "You ought to go" or "He's waiting." As the two of them lay in bed smoking, Hélène said, "You can't let this go on, Max."

"What? Let what go on?"

And she would've preferred not to have to spell it out, hoping that some part of him was prepared to hear it, so that she wouldn't have to say names she didn't want to say, and did leave left unsaid, not jabbing his flesh with them. Sitting on the edge of the bed as she began to get dressed, she just said, "You're a pain in the ass, Max," while a kind of worried darkness rose in his mind, getting blacker and blacker, sort of like the sun covered by the moon during a total eclipse.

"My daughter's grown up," he said, "she does what she wants."

And as Hélène fastened the last buttons on her blouse, she said, "Yeah, you're probably right, so long as nobody knows about it."

Max suddenly sat up in bed, frowning. "Nobody knows what?"

At that moment, Hélène realized that they weren't talking about the same thing. Max accepted the fact that his daughter was working for Franck Bellec as a barmaid, but that was it. He didn't know anything else, didn't suspect anything else, didn't imagine anything else, the way people can sometimes keep certain things buried and invisible. But Hélène didn't need to say anything more, because in his skull, Max was running through the possibilities, and among those possibilities, of course, was the worst one.

"What are you trying to tell me, Hélène?" And because she didn't answer, because she couldn't, he grabbed her arm and repeated, "What are you trying to tell me?"

She pulled her arm free and backed away, saying only, "I'm... I'm so sorry, there was nothing I could do."

Max tried to conceive the hypothesis he had glimpsed—because it was just a hypothesis, right? It had to be just a hypothesis, and as such, Max could refute it by slowly twisting it, the way you might ruin an iron rod, because he knew Hélène, who always went for the dramatic, and Franck would never let that happen, and Laura had a good head on her shoulders. And Max continued twisting the iron rod, refusing to see the man he drove every day and his own daughter together in the same room, keeping them apart like two distinct bubbles separating the man in the back of his car and his daughter, Laura, so it was impossible to bring them close enough together, like on a visit to the orthoptist where you're supposed to move the image of the animal into the circle. Well, it was the same thing here, if the circle was the mayor and the animal was his daughter, he could never put her in that circle. And because of this glaringly obvious truth, this intuition he couldn't avoid, Max suddenly felt as if he had isolated it in a well-fenced park within himself, like a cage that he watched over with his back turned. He didn't know that while he stood guard in front of the steel barrier, the beast was digging and digging behind him. And it probably dug one of the finest tunnels in the world, until it came out in broad daylight right where he was standing guard, whispering to his face, Of course you've known it for a long time, you just didn't want to see it: Your daughter has become your boss's whore.

And all that, all those thoughts spinning around a thousand times, lasted maybe a quarter of a second, the time it took for Max to lift the sheet off himself and sit on the edge of the bed, with a silent Hélène at his side. He got dressed slowly, mechanically, and went out into the breaking day with the sad blue of dawn enveloping everything, the city, the sea, his soul, walking on the beach without even glancing at it, moving like an automaton that knows what it has to do.

He walked under the city hall portico and over to his car in the parking lot. He glanced at the seagull shit on the rear fender. It's true, he told himself, the car's dirty, it needs to be washed. And that's what he did. He got behind the wheel. He took off. He drove to the nearest car wash. He drove the car onto the rails. He stepped out and put a coin in the machine's slot. He pushed the green button and then, ignoring the prohibition printed in red letters, got back inside. The attendant in his booth supervising the car wash came out yelling, and rapped on the closed window to tell him to get out, but Max didn't move, and the man jumped away, so as not to also be dragged along as the wheels started to move on the tracks, as the first jets of warm water started obscuring the windshield, soon followed by white foam that grayed out the light, and which Max would have liked to see seep into the car, the way when you're exhausted you sometimes let yourself slide to the bottom of a full bathtub. Then the big black brushes worked their way along the car body to the rear fender, washing the seagull shit away. Max got out of the car, checked to see that everything was clean, and took off. From the now gleaming limousine, he could see the big billboards lining the avenues like shoots of metal and glass that hoped to rival the plane trees, could see the posters announcing his next fight, two men with raised fists silhouetted against the starry background, with "BIG BOXING MATCH, SATURDAY, APRIL 5" in bold letters.

Except that April 5 was tomorrow.

PART TWO

1

Lying semiconscious and glassy-eyed, Max moved out of the arena in slow motion, on a swaying stretcher surrounded by faces. He saw their mouths all shaping big letters and yelling, but a kind of cotton partition seemed to separate him from the world, and he didn't hear anything. He could barely make out Laura, who wouldn't let go of his hand, as if her hand were keeping him in the world of the living. Looking at her lips, he guessed she was saying the usual things you say in these situations, his name over and over, then, "Hang in there, Dad. Hang on," amid the same muffled noise, while using all her strength to protect him from the press of people crowding around them, especially the photographers who kept raising their cameras and endlessly firing flashes down at his broken body. Beyond them, the five hundred spectators still in semidarkness didn't understand—couldn't understand—why Max hadn't been the one raising his arms very high over the lighted ring in a victory they had all expected from him. Instead it was Costa, seven years his junior, who'd probably thought his life wasn't worth a plug nickel when he stepped into the ring twenty minutes earlier, and still couldn't believe he had really watched Max Le Corre crumble under his punches.

How could all those spectators know why Max's legs seemed to buckle under the weight of his torso, why his face offered itself so freely to the power of his opponent's gloves. He'd suddenly been as frail as a candle flame blown on by a child, briefly flickering at the edge of extinction until the flame gave up and Max collapsed, first staggering, then falling, having stumbled around the ring as long as he could, his legs like ninepins wobbling for a moment before toppling over, one hand still clinging to a rope, then letting go as well. Even the referee didn't dare start the count too soon, sure that at any moment Max would get up and finish the fight. But as he lay on the stretcher, the rest of the fight was now between him and his daughter, and first consisted in gathering the shards of reality scattered through the air like broken window glass and mixed by the crowd, the way you might imagine a rowboat in rough seas, knocked about by the unpredictable rhythm of the EMTs pushing their way through the crowd as it surged this way and that, sweeping everyone along in a shared sea of random motions, as if crowds had a life of their own, a life that you shared in the plural when you abandoned your body to all of ours without distinction, everyone moved by a collective tectonic and confused spirit, each person realizing that joining or leaving was no longer up to them, or even to fight for a bit of breathing room, but that the time had come to slip blindly into the wave and be carried by it.

On the stretcher, Max no longer felt the loneliness of defeat, or even the diffuse pain in his bones, but a strange floating bath of ether from which he almost smiled at them all, the photographers, Laura, and even Franck, even horrible Franck, who looked at Max's battered face with the fatalism of someone who is master of the situation, the kind of look that compassion, goodwill, and even friendship had long since deserted. And Laura kept saying, "It'll be okay, Dad. You'll pull through." Seated in the front row, she had seen that moment when something in her father's body stopped, as if the earth had suddenly opened under his feet while the other man pounded away, unleashing hooks and punches with Max against the ropes, his face almost welcoming the punishment, unable to respond anymore, barely able to keep his hands up to protect himself. It was as if a crevasse had yawned open, the sort of thing that happens when hiking on a glacier in the high mountains.

She had tried to see him before the fight, to visit him in the locker room and wish him good luck. His hands were already wrapped in white gauze and he was wearing the robe embroidered with his name that he had kept from his younger days. He was warming up one last time before slipping on his gloves, and had arranged it so as not to see her. He had asked that no one bother him before he headed down the long hallway and out into the lights, with the ring's ropes in the distance like the rigging of a ship on which he was embarking for a long voyage.

So Laura went to her reserved seat in the front row in the hot arena, with Franck Bellec on one side and Quentin Le Bars on the other. The latter was tempted to put his hand on her thigh in the darkness, but of course he didn't, not in front of the five hundred people who saw them greet each other and probably found it normal that the two should know each other and would come to such an event together. If it had been up to Laura, she wouldn't have asked to be put next to him, but she wasn't the person choosing the arena's seating plan, that was Franck, and Franck obeyed the mayor, and the mayor obeyed his desire.

Franck and Laura were both already seated when Le Bars arrived. Franck stood up to shake hands, gave him a big smile, and said, "How are you, Mr. Minister?" Laura's head snapped around to Franck with a questioning expression he must have expected. What, didn't he tell you? As Le Bars sat down, he whispered in her ear, "It isn't official yet, but yes, I'm going to be named a cabinet minister."

She didn't know what to think and wanted to understand what this would change for her, but as Le Bars looked at the ring, he added, "You'll come see me in Paris," as if it were obvious. The sound from the loudspeaker was already drowning out his voice, announcing the entrance of the two boxers who stepped under the ropes together and waved confidently to the crowd, their bodies facing each other, itching to get started, fighting already, as the referee intoned the few ritual sentences, to fight according to the rules and to listen to the referee, but they themselves didn't hear, looking into each other's face as though to lose themselves in it, to drive away any thought that would suspend the moment, any thought that would pull Max away from what was now his only task: to quiet the echo chamber of his brain, whose walls could start interfering at any moment, when what mattered was the most direct route from brain to hands, ignoring even the rumbling of the sea and the murmur from the rear bleachers, the chanting of his name buzzing in his temples, as if a too-hot wind were blowing in his face. And the bell to start the first round hadn't even rung when Max already knew, or something in him knew, that he was going to lose. Perched like a bird in its nest, he forced himself not to look down at the audience, not to see his own daughter settled between her two executioners, the three who together would witness the disaster, that is, see him get destroyed in the third of the anticipated twelve rounds.

And Laura screamed with all her might, demanding that the fight be stopped when she saw that he kept insisting—not Costa, who was throwing the punches, but Max—insisting on getting up before the end of each countdown, as if he hadn't taken enough, trapped against the ropes and getting seven, eight punches that whipped his head from side to side like an overripe fruit being crushed, his face more and more bloody, looking like he expected death itself under the glare of the lights. At one point—and she was never sure of this—she thought she saw him give her almost a smile, yes, she thought she saw that he was smiling while being pounded, when he could have simply dropped to the canvas and ended it all, but seemed to actually want more and more.

Next to Laura, Le Bars hesitated, wanting to take her hand, to tell her, "Calm down." He might even have wanted to say "My love" or "Darling," suddenly ejected from his official position by her tears and the distress wracking her body as Max kept asking for more, having fallen three times and gotten up three times, as if something in him demanded to be hit again and again, taking three extra rounds for the same result, the defeat written in his mind. But it was only in his mind, I mean. Costa, his opponent, didn't know it, couldn't know it, so he kept punching with all his might. With a right uppercut he drove the bone in Max's nose all the way into his brain, and Max couldn't help but crumple, without anyone knowing how long he would take to get back up, but certainly much longer than the official ten seconds. Even with the most generous, partial referee on the planet, willing to stretch out the seconds to double length, there wouldn't have been enough time for the shattered man to get up. For Max, his unseeing gaze lost in the vast confusion of the arena and the brouhaha turned to cotton that kept suffocating him like a pillow pressed on his face, everything fused together at that moment without his ever knowing exactly when the first crack, breach, or fault had opened in him, brushing him like a cold draft from the locker room, perhaps, blowing that black-magic dust on his gloves so that what fell to the canvas wasn't only Max's weary body but the compressed version of his existence, the way a lightbulb filament that has exhausted its strength will suddenly snap.

As she walked along beside the stretcher, Laura couldn't see all that, only the limp body with the thousand shocks it had suffered, much too groggy to tell which part of his face or body hurt so much. Despite the slaps that the medic kept giving him to make him keep his eyes open, Max felt that his lids were as heavy as lead shoes, while something that you might call soul or spirit, something was detaching itself from him. Though still lying prone, he suddenly saw everyone from above, the melee of heads clustered around him and rumbling like a storm and the lightning-like flashes striking everywhere, while he kept climbing higher and higher, like smoke rising to the ceiling and filling the entire arena, as the strange clamor kept up, maybe hesitant to salute Costa's victory as he paraded around the ring stepping in the still-damp blood on the canvas, stunned by this victory that was so easy and so unexpected, the kind of victory that boxing doesn't forget, just as it remembers things that are out of the ordinary in fights, quick to mythify all those occasions where something finally happens, for better or for worse. And outside, as the stretcher was being lifted into the ambulance, Max glimpsed the suddenly ironic poster on the front of the arena he'd just exited, showing him standing and determined, above his name in big letters, his gaze inhabited by some savage animal that served as his totem. He was staring at the camera with all his weight, all his muscles, all that power that he had learned to project at the sight of a photographer and which that evening, in spite of the hundreds of flashes fired at him, had dissolved in the arena. And then, as if that power on display made too stark a contrast with his condition on the stretcher, as if his entire life was slipping into the interval, he passed out.

2

nly Laura remembered the trip to the hospital, the nighttime city flashing by the opaque windows in streaks of light, covered by the sound of the siren that seemed to be telling everyone that Max Le Corre, the boxing champion they had admired all these years, was finished, in the very city where by cruel irony the shameful bout took place under the eyes of hundreds of friends and admirers who had bet on him, including some who'd placed huge wagers on his winning. And Laura was there when he opened his eyes in a room haunted by his long sleep, sitting in the corner of the white wall, daylight from the window falling on the lines of the newspaper she was reading. Without moving, Max realized that he had woken up, and asked what time it was. He didn't yet know that what was important at that moment wasn't the time but the date, since it was eight days later.

Laura told him this later still, describing the long week when he hadn't opened an eye or said a word, put in an artificial sleep to let him rest from all the blows that had rattled his body and brain and left him in a kind of coma, absent from the world. She had strained to believe that some part of him was still sentient and hearing her, even though he wasn't responding. Which is why she read the local newspaper to him every day from the first page to the last, without paying attention to what she was reading or saying: news items, the state of the market, everything that had happened in the world and the city, without distinction. She didn't even spare him the account of his own fight, hoping that the reporters' suspicious, angry, or insulting comments might shock his sleeping consciousness, that he would jerk upright and immediately start planning a rematch. She knew he was capable of that kind of anger, and hoped that by mocking his masculinity, she would see him suddenly sit up in his bed, already preparing for his imminent comeback. Because there's no boxing without anger, is there? Yet that innermost part of him seemed to have collapsed, like an unexpected market crash that devastates the New York or London stock exchanges. The same was true of his anger, which had sunk to its lowest ebb—unless it was just being redirected, which was something Laura didn't know yet. She didn't know that Max's opponent with the strong jaw and oiled body wasn't the enemy to be defeated, because the enemy now wore a black suit and a different tie every day, the enemy Max had had within range of his fists for months, yet Max had smiled at him and driven him around the city, bringing him his daughter's head on a silver platter a little more each day.

And among the news stories that Laura read aloud in the white room, one that also failed to wake her father was that Quentin Le Bars had been named a minister, that he had met the president in person yesterday evening and declared himself proud of the responsibility he was being given, in this case the Ministry of Maritime Affairs, making him the minister of the sea. This was a position he had schemed to get for so many months, pulling every string and drawing on every single connection and source of support, gradually making himself look like the right man for the job.

When Laura read that about Le Bars, she couldn't help interrupting her reading, not because she was surprised (she already knew it) but because when she saw it on the front page of a newspaper she'd known since she was a child, in a full-page photograph with the president of the Republic, a kind of seemingly impossible telescoping happened in her mind, as she first remembered his naked body when he was under her, then saw him in his tailored suit on the front steps of the Élysée Palace—it was something she couldn't conceive of.

"I don't know what went through my mind," she told the policemen. "Maybe just realizing that only a little handshake connected me with the president of the Republic, and that hand belonged to the man who had been visiting me for weeks."

In any case, she put down the newspaper, took out her phone, and started to type the message onscreen she would send spontaneously, as it were, to the new minister, unable to weigh how much irony, bitterness, and at the same time sincerity was involved. She simply wrote, "Bravo for your appointment, Laura."

The two policemen listening to her once again looked as if they had gotten an electric shock. One sat back in his chair; the other, unable to contain himself, said, "You texted him, the minister? To his cell phone?"

She nodded yes, still surprised at what she had done, while the policemen exchanged a glance and sighed deeply, looking as if they had just lost their judgment.

"What? Didn't I have the right to do that, either?"

"It isn't a matter of right," said one of them, "but things like that don't help your case. It's the kind of information that certain people hanging out hallways are always listening for."

"Snoops, basically," added the other cop.

"Maybe, but at that level I wouldn't call them snoops," she said. "I'd call them shit pickers."

"Saying that doesn't help you."

"I'm not here to help myself."

The two men grinned at each other again, recognizing her determination and maybe also trying to imagine Le Bars's expression when he got Laura's message. It was certainly worth imagining.

So there's Le Bars around eleven o'clock on Wednesday morning, attending his first Council of Ministers, with his phone lying on the long meeting table, and suddenly he sees it light up, displaying the word "Laura." It jolts him like the sting of a jellyfish or a wasp, and he slaps his hand on the phone so a minister sitting next to him can't see the name, never mind the message. Because that name, "Laura," is the open sesame to an intimate world, a yawning gap away from the present and whose depth Le Bars is now trying to fathom. Worse, it's a kind of shadow, a sword of Damocles over his head, as he now imagines her satisfaction, the discreet–and latent, for now–form of the power she suddenly has over him, to the point that he even stops listening to the president, who is making the rounds of the newcomers at the table. Caught in the web of his own surprise, Le Bars hesitates about what course to take. Answer her, or not? Refuse any contact, or string her along? That's it, he thinks, promise her anything, say that of course he hasn't forgotten her and that he's fond of her, and hopes they can go on seeing each other. All these ideas come together in an open and almost complicit formula that he discreetly types on his screen: "Thanks Laura. See you soon, I hope," and sends, without even knowing, as he is writing, whether he believes a single word of it.

It was only later, when Le Bars had left the presidential palace and was being driven through the streets of Paris in a car even blacker and bigger than the one before, that he thought to himself, Well, it's not that bad, and Maybe I can see her again, after all, in that almost abstract and certainly impressive way she had flashed through his memory, and which was nothing other than the grip of a desire.

Still sitting in the hospital room with Le Bars's name displayed over the words "See you soon," Laura didn't try to gauge how much sincerity he'd put in it, but suddenly felt almost flattered, in a way.

"Yeah, I won't deny it," she said. "I felt important that day."

3

he didn't notice right away that Max had woken up. His eyes were wide open, but he didn't move—his head was held in a neck brace—just kept on repeating, in a weak, anxious voice: "The car's clean now, you can tell him it's clean." Laura leaped up, took his hand, and said, "Yes, the car is clean, don't worry." The doctor was soon on his way, alerted by the nurse who had heard Laura from the other hallway and told him that the boxer in Number 12 was awake. Said doctor entered the room with the somewhat casual manner that all doctors in all hospitals have, of creating an instant connection with patients whose name they hadn't known a moment before. In this case, it was, "So, Mr. Le Corre, are you feeling better? Ready to climb back into the ring?" In a show of complicity or comfort, he tried to mime throwing a punch, and Max forced an answering smile. The doctor put his hands in his lab-coat pockets and nodded to Laura to join him in the hallway, the way all doctors do when they have bad news to announce without the patient knowing. She followed him out, and listened.

"Your father is damaged, and he has lesions in his brain," he said, showing her scans of Max's cerebral activity. "It's not clear that he'll regain all his faculties. His nerves have been severely tested, as you can see.

"That's a known risk for boxers. The more punches they take, the more likely they are to become demented or brain damaged. And as they get older, a kind of opaque glass forms between them and the world. All they can make out through it are shadows, just volumes and shapes, like some animals at night, supposedly.

"It's the same with beekeepers," the doctor continued. "They get stung by their bees thousands of times while collecting honey, but they hardly feel it, because they're so used to being stung. But then a day comes with one sting too many, and they drop dead. That's the way it is with boxers. They take hard punches every day but seem immune to them, and almost indifferent, but like termites gnawing, every punch does its bit of damage. Then one day the boxer takes one little jab or one uppercut too many, and he falls down and doesn't get up."

"I know my father," said Laura. "He didn't want to go on boxing. He won't miss it."

"You don't seem to understand, miss. He won't be able to go back to his job at city hall, either. He'll have to find some other work."

And Max, maybe because he could hear the conversation in the distance, or maybe because he heard the word "work," or maybe because he was moving in a parallel world, went on repeating, in a half sleep: "The car's clean, Mr. Mayor, perfectly clean. I swear."

Laura and the doctor reentered the room to find him smiling from the calm of the sheets. They were a bit scratchy and worn, but a softer carapace than the walls of his home, if you could even say he still had a home, that is, because it seemed to have become very far away, but in any case was now no longer made of bricks and stone but of some threadbare fabric that could rip at any moment, split at the least breath of wind or stroke of a knife. "So there's no question of him resuming a normal life," the doctor continued. "Your father isn't ready," he said, then added, "He may never be ready."

As he walked away, she went to sit in the only chair near the bed and said, "Everything's fine, Dad. You'll be outside soon." She turned on the television and briefly fiddled with the remote as the little wall-mounted screen produced afternoon soap operas, stupid games, and regional network news.

That's when she saw him: Quentin Le Bars, the minister of maritime affairs, crossing the Élysée Palace courtyard with a briefcase under his arm, like all ministers, and waving at every single camera. To Laura, it felt as if he were greeting her personally, saying, "See you soon, I hope" again, and she almost believed it. But there was another person in the room, in bed, who also saw Le Bars. With his eyes on the TV and his neck held rigid by the brace, Max spoke up. In a clearer voice that seemed to summon all his strength, he asked, "Are you going to see him again?"

Laura turned her head toward her father, not sure she had heard right, in the triangle drawn from where he was to the TV screen, and from the screen back to where she was sitting by the bed, the way a bullet from a revolver might ricochet at an acute angle from the screen to hit her somewhere between her temple and her brain. Max was lying helpless in a hospital bed. yet had managed to put everything he knew into those seven words—Are you going to see him again?—everything he seemed to have always known but had locked away for so long in a safe that he was now opening, and put before her in a single charge that threatened to explode. This was just his way of telling her that he knew, and he did it calmly, without anger or cynicism, madness or excess, yet without realizing that he had never struck a blow this hard in a lifetime in the ring. Laura found herself wondering how long he had known, when he had figured it out, now that those seven words had clarified the events of these last days, beginning with the defeat that she now understood all too well.

She might have done what you sometimes do when you think you're telling a lie well, and said, "See who? Who do you mean?" But she didn't. Thrust deep into her interior cylinder, she no longer had the means, and could only try to remember that she hadn't lost the use of language, yet was unable to produce a single verb or noun, or even to stammer a "But..." or a "What do you..." for the good reason that even inside her, even where she had gathered thousands of words a moment before, all the world's languages had fallen into a bottomless well. In her panicky silence, she wasn't even sure of her own answer, she wasn't able to say, or even think,

"That bastard? No, of course not," but rather "Who knows?" or maybe even "Yeah, sure," as if, once out of her father's sight, she was again barricaded against fate, just a girl who wasn't born to make decisions and had been used for so long by people who knew how to make them, despite being clearheaded and capable of plumbing the whole situation, but now feeling dismayed by the sterility of her own intelligence. So it was easier, and also more necessary, to consider that events had just unfolded the way they were supposed to, forgetting what she herself had so long considered to be a trap from which she hadn't managed to escape, trying to tell herself—as if justifying herself before an inner tribunal—from now on, that it was normal, he did me a favor and I did him one, no big deal. This was her way of making peace with it, making prosaic the thing that had so violently connected them—no, not violently, a simple deal, she insisted, just a quid pro quo, and who cares that my own body was at stake instead of money?

Laura didn't tell her father all this, or anything else. She just said, "I'm going, Dad. I'll be back tomorrow." And she thought about what the doctor had told her, that Max would never return to a normal life, neither to the ring nor to the routine he had lived all these years at the wheel of the municipal limousine. She imagined him slowly wasting away in a nursing home, unemployed before his time and sinking into alcoholic stupors in his sleepless nights.

"So yeah, I figured there might be a solution," she told the policemen.

"A solution?"

"Yes, one final arrangement."

In the long hallway leading out of the hospital, Laura did this crazy thing, took out her phone and wrote to Le Bars, "When can we get together?"

"Yeah, I'm the one who started it up again," she said. "I won't ever deny it." As she watched, the cop focused on his computer screen was looking at her less and less, whereas the other one, who was still standing, almost sighed, or at least breathed more heavily, as if to signify his disapproval.

"But going back to someone who has controlled you is just Psychology 101, isn't it?" said Laura.

"I thought you hadn't studied psychology?"

"That doesn't mean I don't know things."

4

he told them about her trip to Paris, of course, which had given her the feeling she'd had when she was a little girl bent on running away, a thing she had endlessly planned but never carried out, keeping a bag packed and ready behind her bedroom door for so many years. How often had she checked to make sure it held everything she needed? Money, of course, and a wool sweater, a change of socks, a flashlight, some cookies, and some new notebooks and pens so she could keep a journal. Every night when she went to sleep, she made a list of everything she would need to survive the coming days, because at dawn she would be far away, and when her parents said good night it was for the last time, though they didn't know it. So when she saw herself at breakfast the next morning, it was strange, having another girl at her place who had forgotten she was supposed to leave, even forgotten the existence of a bag that from her morning perch she now viewed with condescension, as if tapping her on the shoulder and saying, "Poor girl, how naïve you still are."

And how naïve Laura still was in leaping into action when Le Bars answered her text an hour later, suggesting a date, like "Tomorrow?" To which she wrote, "OK tomorrow. I'll buy my ticket."

On the train taking her to Paris the next day, she watched the power lines undulate along the rails, already imagining their meeting in this new setting. She had her doubts, of course, fooling herself about how she felt about herself and what she was about to do, telling herself that it was just an arrangement, one last deal, and then it would be over. She almost wanted to tell her story to her fellow travelers, saying, "Yes, I'm going to Paris, I'm going to spend the night with Quentin Le Bars, the new minister. Yes, but our relationship is complicated," suddenly convinced that the entire train car was pondering her case and whispering, "Yes, that's her, that's Le Bars's mistress, I recognize her," the way we sometimes think that instead of a God observing us there's only the concentrated muttering of five billion people, all with their eyes turned to us. That's absurd, of course, but that's the way it is, and even though she tried to not think what she was thinking, tried to tell herself that she going there mainly for her father, to get Le Bars to do something for her father, the thought kept coming back. Because we're never able to completely untangle ourselves from the black knot of certain actions that drive us.

She was the one who booked the hotel, searching on the Internet for something not too expensive but decent enough to receive him, settling for a two-star hotel in the suburbs, not too far out, but discreet enough so he wouldn't feel uncomfortable. In giving her name to the reservation desk she was tempted to say, "Yes, Le Corre, like the boxer," but didn't. Instead, she said, "A double room. My husband is already in Paris, he'll join me a little later."

They had also agreed that she would be there before him, so he could head right upstairs without going by the front desk, maybe just calling from the hallway, "I'm in Room 28," as she had texted him, "Room 28. I'll leave the door unlocked." So she went up and waited for him. From the window, she looked out at the tower blocks and the ring road in the distance, lost in an unfamiliar suburb, with her phone as her only guidepost or compass, on which he'd texted, "I'll be there around 7."

In the taxi bringing Le Bars there, he realized it had been a long time since he'd been this far outside Paris, and that in his own eyes he had never fallen so low in society. Even when the taxi dropped him in front of the hotel, his having to venture out alone beyond the ring roads without an assistant or a bodyguard, like some commuter heading home, felt a bit humiliating. He was also feeling tense with desire, almost a slave to his memory of her body, a slave to all those times he could visualize himself coming on her belly or in her mouth, and wondering which he would choose that day, as if he were going to a restaurant and hesitating over the menu. While those lubricious thoughts occupied Le Bars's mind, Laura was putting on mascara, hoping to lengthen her eyelashes a little more, while the word "minister" kept echoing in her mind. She wasn't able to think "Le Bars," unable to forget that she was receiving a minister in this new room in a new city. This was totally different from the first times, of course, and of course he would help her, just a couple of phone calls and Max would get a job at city hall again. Le Bars couldn't put her off this time, she was willing to forget his promise to get her an apartment, but yes, he could do something for her father. He may be a minister, she thought, but he wasn't a monster for all that.

"That was yet to be proved, though," she told the policemen. "When I saw him come in and close the door behind him, I realized right away that the only thing that had entered the room was his desire, and also his pride, which would settle into the armchair at the foot of the bed and watch him lie down and untie his tie, the way you might look at a drunk in the street. He hardly spoke to me, just being polite, saying, 'How are you? I'm glad to see you again.' As he stretched out, half naked and with his belt already unbuckled, he added, 'I don't have much time.'

"Yeah, I understood right away," she said. "I mean not what was going to happen—I knew that already—but all those false hopes that I'd had, the idea that it could be, I don't know, friendly."

"Friendly?"

"Yeah, friendly. I thought that. Crazy isn't it? But it wasn't like that at all, I just got undressed while he watched and I did what I had to do."

"Did you talk to him about your father?"

"No, not right away. But when it was all over a few minutes later, when he was pulling up his pants, I remember it perfectly, I said, 'Quentin—' "

And she wondered how many times she had dared to use his first name. Once or twice, maybe, and he was surprised and annoyed that, given his new position, she would drag him into the intimacy of a first name, especially now that his desire was spent, a dead thing, and his very presence here, in this fleabag hotel, was practically making him nauseous.

"I wanted to ask you something," she finally said. "It's for my father."

"Ah, yes, your father. How is he?"

"I wondered if you might be able to help, ask city hall if they could give him a job or..."

He looked at her with that phony compassion that borders on contempt, telling himself, She doesn't get it, doesn't see the die was cast a long time ago. Which was just a way of thinking, Why should I stick my neck out to help some poor guy who can't help himself? He didn't mean only the lost boxing match but the whole drive to failure or impotence that Max seemed prey to—the kind of psychology Le Bars avoided like the plague.

And because at that point they understood each other faster than the sentences they would shape, he cut to the chase. He said, "Nowadays, I can't afford to—"

"Maybe just a phone call," she said.

"No, it would get back to me. I can't do it."

Her request probably wound up hastening his departure, and he got up the moment the conversation took this overly serious turn. He tucked his shirt into his pants, pulled his belt a notch tighter, and apologized at having to leave so soon while pulling on his jacket. He forced himself to kiss her on the forehead and then, trying to lighten the mood, smiled and said, "Please excuse me,

I'm as busy as a cabinet minister!" And she watched him leave.

"Maybe you should've talked to him before," said one policeman.

"Before what?"

What could the cop say? Before having sex, before making love? That for a favor like that, she should have asked beforehand, when his cock's work was yet to be accomplished? But no, that wouldn't have changed anything, he would have just lied a little more to get what he wanted. He would have said, "Oh sure, of course," almost automatically, the way he might slip a fifty-euro bill into her back pocket, except that maybe he thought she should pay him, in any case that was the feeling she had when she left the room, with him already long gone. When she handed in the key at the front desk and was about to say goodbye, the receptionist told her, "You need to pay for the room, miss."

"Yeah, he did that too," she told the cops. "The bastard made me pay for the room."

5

All this burned like a spark in Laura's mind while on the train ride home, covering two hundred and fifty miles with a taste of sperm still in her mouth that no coffee from the TGV bar could wash away. The kind of taste that your brain can re-create for days on end, for the sole pleasure either of wallowing in the mistake or maybe of keeping the anger alive. And in a way, so much the better. In a way, it's good that the body remembers, and screams at being poisoned while it's making you vomit in the train toilet.

When she returned from Paris, when she got off the train that day, set foot on the station platform and crossed the hall to the big forecourt, Laura instinctively headed for the shore far from the walled city, which no longer concerned her, any more than the tall ships in the big basins, ghost mummies that had sailed their way uninvited into the layout of the harbor.

The sky was wide and gray, an almost pearl color and practically motionless, without a drop of rain or breath of wind, the kind of nacreous, cotton-like sky that leaves the sea darker, barely gleaming and as opaque as it is wont to be in a dead calm. Laura went down to the beach and deliberately walked fast, sinking into the sand, breathing deeply and feeling her head get dizzy with oxygen. Behind the fog of her eyes lay only the badly stratified memory of her sleepless night, with all the anger mixed with fatigue that had overtaken her long before dawn, that is, long before leaving that hotel room where Le Bars had spent exactly nineteen minutes, she noted, before leaving her on that neutral tone that self-confident people have, maybe telling her, "Let me know the next time you're in Paris," while he finished tying his shoelaces, then picked up his wallet from the night table before vanishing in the sharp click of the closing door. I don't know what she said or thought at that moment, but I imagine she was astonished to see him get dressed so fast, as she measured all the energy she had invested on getting there, the money spent on her train ticket, and the nervous time, now wasted, watching the western plains roll by, her anger rising with every passing mile. And in a way, so much the better.

So much the better that some days in our lives are like tipping points, crests beyond which we're aware that the sea below us is breaking on rocky crags, and that some days, yes, some days have to be handled cautiously, the way you round a dangerous cape. Laura had already rounded a few capes in her life, and not with what I would call complete clarity or even complete caution, but despite her youth, she had kept a weather eye out, watching as if from the highest crow's nest on a mast she was erecting, and even slowly climbing, to survey the water around her. Except that until a certain age we live in a fog that is hard to pierce, the kind that cuts off any view of a future, and not just the future but even the past, the very shadow of what we have lived through, so we can't count on memory or experience to project ourselves onto tomorrow, and because until a certain age we put up with the fog, strangely enough, we put up with not seeing very far, we settle for the limited perimeter of what we can see, or, better yet, we don't even realize that a world without fog exists, but what happens is that at some point, we realize that a different weather, a different sky, must exist, or in any case we demand it, and in demanding it, well, in demanding it we start slashing the air with sharp weapons. So when Laura felt she was drained by all her laborious steps on the beach, when she had yelled her fill at the sea, she turned around, climbed up to the road, and this time walked along the old city ramparts to police headquarters. Without hesitation, she walked through the gate and crossed the courtyard, to go stand at the front desk where the duty officer was already watching her, and said, "I want to file a complaint."

6

In trying to explain it later, Laura said it felt as if a giant hand on her back had pushed her, or a wave taller than the others had taken her by the arm and raised her higher than she'd expected. And bursting from that wave was no covey of smirking sea naiads but Nemesis herself, come to bestow the quasi-pneumatic force that Laura felt had deposited her there, on the steps in front of police headquarters. And it gave the duty officer a very odd feeling to hear the name Le Bars, after he'd mindlessly asked, "File a complaint? Right. Against who?"

Aware of the effect she was having, Laura said, "Le Bars." At that, the cop's eyes brightened, or widened, and she could tell that he'd immediately moved into his body, as if a ventriloquist had been speaking through him up to then, using the voice we all have for everyday situations, until something happens or a wire is suddenly plugged in, and everything changes and starts to hum. He said, "One moment, please." Laura watched him leave through the glass door behind him to go talk with a man sitting in an office who was clearly his superior and who wheeled around to look at her through the glass. She couldn't hear their conversation, just tried to read their lips while she watched their frowns deepen, as if they had both quickly realized the heavens were falling on their heads. The desk sergeant returned and asked her to come around the counter into the glassed-in office. He closed the door behind her and hung up a sign that read "INTERVIEW IN PROGRESS." The seated cop waved Laura to a chair. Facing her and his computer screen, he pulled the keyboard closer and limbered his fingers, the way a surgeon might prepare his instruments before operating. Or at least that's the way Laura experienced it, that she had been rolled into an operating room on a gurney with barely time to glimpse the scalpel and the lancet, ready to yield to the sleep of anesthesia. Except that this time the anesthesia was more like a hypnosis session where you start telling your story, an endless half sleep where she felt she was nothing but a cadaver on one those old anatomy charts, and the long skein of her story was being extirpated from the jungle of organs serving as her body and extruded from her lips. It was exactly the contrary of the endurance that she had displayed during those weeks spent holding the sentences inside herself, keeping them in a larval, inarticulate state and denying them access to the light of language. And now it was like her story was no longer her own, and actually that was why she was there, to tell her story in the third person, imagining herself standing next to the surgeon, assisting him like a scrub nurse, describing the facts, even those she couldn't qualify as criminal, not speaking of rape or procuring, much less influence peddling or undue duress, just describing in order the insidious and growing hold he'd had on her.

"But having a hold on someone isn't a crime, is it?" she asked.

"That depends, it's possible," said the policeman as he watched the pages emerge from his printer before asking her to reread her account. As if waking from the long amnesia that Le Bars seemed to have produced, and realizing for the first time that she had turned the entire path that had led to her own present into written sentences, Laura nearly started, and said, "Reread it? Why?"

"That's the rule, miss. You have to read it before signing it," he said, handing her the printout. And as she read it over, she was even more aware that each "I" punctuating her story had changed into a "she," almost unable to join the two now-separated instances. She felt like a stranger looking at this girl named Laura who was declaring on her honor the truth of the aforementioned facts. As she handed the signed document to the police officer, she couldn't help asking, "Do you think he'll be convicted?"

"He'd have to be indicted first. There would be an investigation."

"Yeah, but he'll be convicted in the end, won't he?" she insisted.

"It's a delicate matter. I'm not a judge." As he walked her to the door, he added, "I would advise you to get a lawyer."

That was certainly one of the best pieces of advice he could have given her. As she disappeared through the police station's automatic doors, the place went to battle stations, as the cop, who had watched the pages filled with words like "sex," "fellatio," and "consent" emerge one by one from the printer, quickly strode down the old building's faded hallways to the prosecutor's office, holding the pages in question as if they were a hand grenade, as if the entire story had been engraved on a white-hot sheet of iron already giving off a sickening burned stench, and the best way to get rid of it was to quickly put the freshly printed transcript under the eyes of the prosecutor in person.

Which is what the cop did, entering the prosecutor's office and setting the three pages in front of him with such a serious expression that the other man immediately understood not what was happening but that *something* was happening, that he had to read it right away. And the cop stood there, following the prosecutor's eyes as they moved from line to line as though he were reading a gripping novel while the man standing waited for him to give his opinion, like a publisher about a manuscript. And the prosecutor did express an opinion when he said, "What is this shit?" in the somewhat stiff and bitter tone of someone who already knows that he's going to be rapped on the knuckles, almost suggesting to the cop that he hadn't done his job correctly, that you don't just register any old complaint like this, that he should have immediately consulted with him, the prosecutor, who would have been happy to see this girl and reason with her, not that he was actually on the other side of the law, but he was the kind of person who preferred arrangement to scandal, who wanted everyone in the little world he felt responsible for to get along, yes, that was the sort of expression that he might use, "What I like, is for everyone to get along." In that sense, in judicial matters you should always measure the costs before the benefits because there's always a risk of trying to explode too many old habits—explode, that's the word—because he felt that what he had under his eyes wasn't just a grenade but a little bomb like you see in comic strips, a black ball with a long fuse that he sensed had already started to burn.

He told the cop to leave him alone, that he would study the situation, the kind of very delicate situation that a prosecutor only faces two or three times in his life, at a point when he doesn't yet know which way the wind will be blowing, whether to dismiss the case without further action or to launch an investigation. He knew that he would forever be "the man who..." meaning the person whose decision, whatever it was, would always be stamped on his brow, something like, "Remember, in the Le Bars affair, he was the man who..." And perhaps telling himself, as he wiped the sweat starting to bead on his forehead, that on the day when he'd felt so proud to be taking his oath, he also should have thought of the casuistry involved. He mentally ran through all the elements of the offenses that Laura's story brought to mind, "sexual extortion," "undue duress," "influence peddling," even "procuring," while reminding himself to tear the paper where he was writing all this down into little pieces and throw them in the trash. He continued searching the list of facts to determine the charges that would be the easiest to bear—not for the accused but for himself—and how he could keep both his job and his integrity. He stood up and paced the squeaky old parquet floor of his office, and sat down again, wondering which among all those crimes were the ones that public opinion would best tolerate, out of ignorance or weariness, the ones whose elements were the vaguest, the most abstract, the most opaque, and the broadest. The following day, the prosecutor opened a preliminary investigation for influence peddling.

7

It's a known fact that when it comes to power, panic increases the closer you get to the top, either because high-ranking figures tend to think that if something manages to reach them, the fate of all humanity must be at stake, or because nothing annoys them more than being caught up in the trivia of the world they forgot they once belonged to. Which was how Le Bars felt when the prosecutor phoned him personally, saying things like "I'm very sorry to bother you with this," and "We know about this kind of girl," but "We're sure it will all work out."

"Fine," said Le Bars. "It's good of you to let me know."

As he hung up, he hated himself for a moment, not from a sudden feeling of guilt but for his lack of scope and strategic ability, that the ambition that had led him since childhood hadn't helped him better keep track of his actions. Le Bars found himself alone in an office even bigger than the last one—he had just selected new curtains from a catalog—suddenly imagining himself quickly leaving it to return to his tiny little city. He slammed his fist on his desk, barely restraining himself from yelling words like "bitch" and "pain in the ass." But he quickly recovered, calmed down, and began to think. And in the hours that followed, who knows how many phone calls began to fly in every direction, in a tangle of invisible, quickly intersecting lines between various agencies, from ministry to intelligence service, from intelligence service to attorney general, and from attorney general back to ministry, as if the little bomb that Laura had planted in her town's police station had slowly morphed into a telegraphic wave without anyone—not the cop, the prosecutor, or the intelligence chief, once he was put in the picture—being able to measure how much each telephone answered, each shared exchange of words, each person working at their level helped the fuse burn a little bit more. At the same time, however, they did know what was bound to happen, that the fuse would eventually carry the spark to the powder, and that it would explode, meaning that the affair would reach the public square via that porous gray zone between the law and the press, maybe in one of those bars lining the streets around the courthouse, whereby the gist of a complaint always winds up printed in the daily newspapers.

This particular complaint was no exception to the rule. Within three days, all France had heard about a girl named Laura whom a current minister had abused, and read a shady tale of housing traded for certain little services. So it was battle stations again, but this time in the ministry offices where upright, gray-clad functionaries advised Le Bars to take the initiative, or not advised, rather intimated the order that he explain himself right away and not let rumors destroy him, to reveal himself candidly in newspapers, radio, and television. He was especially not to wall himself up in silence, which would work against him. All this, Le Bars knew how to do, promptly contacting the national radio stations to deliver speeches he'd prepared, how as the mayor of a small city, he was so close to his voters, often knowing them personally, that it exposes you, and sometimes makes you the focus of their anger. He added that the legal system is used to dealing with such situations and is there to separate the wheat from the chaff.

But the reporters insisted. "So you don't deny meeting Laura Le Corre?"

Le Bars hesitated, creating a moment of dead air that in radio seems to last for hours, before saying, "I don't have to explain my connection with Miss Le Corre."

"But do you know her, or not?"

"We've met several times, actually. And I must say that I am all the more disappointed, not to say astonished, because I feel a great deal of respect and friendship for her."

Laura heard this respect and friendship stuff on her radio. Alone in her room, she couldn't think of a comeback, saying only something like, "He's got a lot of nerve," without weighing her understatement, much less imagining that even as Le Bars was leaving the radio station, he was already moving on to the next stage, the one in which all of Laura's indignation rising into the square of sky defined by her Velux skylight would soon be blown away by what would have to be called stupefaction or even alarm. Ensconced in the leather of his ministerial car, Le Bars was dialing the number of his old friend Bellec and had other plans in mind for her.

"It's good to talk to you, Franck."

In Le Bars's eyes, Franck was the man for the situation, an unseen conductor in an orchestra pit so deep that he could lead any symphony without a single spectator anywhere in the great theater of the world being able see the smallest of his gestures.

"I don't think we have a choice anymore," said Le Bars.

"That's for sure," said Franck. "If you still want to, that is."

"It's too late for scruples," said Le Bars.

Ambiguous sentences followed, like "We have to strike while the iron's hot" and "We have a window of opportunity of two or three days," though no one could have understood what the men had in mind from this conversation alone. To do that, you would have had to stick to them like glue from the very start of this business and plant microphones in Bellec's office. Only then could you grasp the kind of triple-blind thinking they were used to, as if they were playing a long game of carom billiards, in which hitting the red ball would bounce it off the cushion to hit the yellow ball, which in turn would wind up striking the white ball—and the white one, of course, was Laura.

"Okay I'll take care of it," said Bellec.

"Let's stay in touch," said Le Bars. And they hung up.

Sitting at his desk, Franck opened the big drawer and pulled out not a revolver but an old men's magazine. He laid it flat on the polished surface in front of him, then turned the pages to the centerfold where Laura Le Corre posed naked under a photographer's flashes, as lascivious as one can be at sixteen. And as he ran his hand over Laura's glossy image, he reflected that yes, they'd been right to scoop her up as she was leaving the high school. He quickly picked up his phone, asked for the editor in chief of the regional newspaper, and offered to messenger over an important document.

Franck probably had a thought for Max—a guilty thought—as he handed the magazine to the messenger who had walked in still wearing his motorcycle helmet to save time, ready to hop on his scooter and head for the *Ouest-France* building. Franck's office, where he heaved his sigh, was dominated by the French champion's boxing gloves on their stand, its walls hung with photographs of the two of them arm in arm smiling at the camera, Franck in his white suit, which in ten years had expanded by a size or two, Max bare-chested, having just won a bout. That's why Franck felt some scruples at the very moment of betraying him. But just as they say there's many a slip twixt the cup and the lip, with some men there's many a mile twixt scruples and morality. With people like Bellec, it even seems that instead of giving rise to morality, the scruples absolve them, as if having a single repentant thought could absolve you of all sin. And Max or no Max, the front page of the next day's *Ouest-France* bore not the provocative photos of Laura, but a bold, suggestive headline: THE LE BARS AFFAIR: SHE WAS POSING NAKED AT 16.

8

hat difference does it make?" Laura asked the lawyer she'd gone to see. "Even if I'd thought of it, even if I thought that the story would come floating up to the surface like some dead guy's clothes, do you think I still wouldn't have filed a complaint?"

"You could have warned me," snapped the lawyer, looking at the *Ouest-France* page in dismay. "I said to tell me everything."

"Yeah, well, I forgot. It happens, right? To forget certain things?"

"Yes, it happens—certain things," he said sarcastically. "Do you know the theory of the perfect victim?"

"No."

"Well, it's exactly the opposite of you. What we need is for you to have lost everything you had, including your virginity, if possible. That's a perfect victim. And that's what you aren't."

You really aren't, the lawyer thought to himself, wondering why he always got stuck with these impossible cases, full of land mines ready to blow up, starting with those photographs, which he imagined were already in the defense's files, or maybe they weren't, because they wouldn't be needed, considering that as with so many shenanigans, the prosecutor was sure to dismiss the case.

"The one thing that might work would be to prove that Bellec is part of a whole system," he added. "Is that common knowledge?"

"Yeah, everybody knows," said Laura. "But when I go into the casino, it feels weird, like I'm stepping into a bubble. Nothing leaks to the outside."

"The other women would have to talk," said the lawyer.

"Dream on," said Laura.

Still, he tried. He contacted the women at the casino one by one, and one by one they said, No, that is, one by one they said they had never seen the mayor on the premises, that it even seemed crazy to imagine a current mayor around the gambling tables. It was as if somebody had programmed them to all say the same thing and to keep quiet the same way. It didn't fool anybody, but it was nothing doing. Even the fact that they used the same phrases, that they were unanimous in saying that in all the time they'd worked there, they swore that nothing like that ever happened, certainly nothing that would be useful legally. They were also perfectly coached into making a few concessions, that of course they occasionally sat with customers and might accept a glass of champagne, and that over the years a customer may have made a proposition, but it never went beyond that. By the time the lawyer got to the third woman who said, "It never went beyond that" in exactly the same tone, he realized he wasn't getting anywhere, that he was dealing with a smoothly running machine that didn't even bother hiding its workings. It was as if Bellec and his cronies weren't afraid to behave openly, knowing how the game was played, knowing that nothing could be done to them, and even the certainty that the women were lying so mechanically meant nothing within the reality of the law. The lawyer had enough experience to know it was pointless to waste time attacking the high wall that Franck Bellec had erected around himself, locking his women in silence and denials.

"This is hopeless," the lawyer said.

"I don't see what difference it makes," Laura repeated.

"The difference is that without a witness and with your naked photos, people's opinion won't be on your side."

"People aren't that stupid," she said.

"No, not that stupid, but old habits die hard."

In a way, he was right. People might call Le Bars a bastard, but they couldn't help calling Laura a slut, and in doing so, put their thumbs on the human-nature side of the scale—the burden of men's insatiable lust and women's shabbiness in taking advantage of it. Those were the sorts of things that would have to be overcome at trial, said the lawyer. "Unspoken things. Especially because he's about to play his trump card."

"What you mean?" asked Laura. "What trump card?"

He slid the *Ouest-France* article on his desk over to her, and Laura learned not only that she was a loose woman but also that Le Bars would soon be visiting his hometown. On the pretext of inaugurating the marina's new docks, he was coming to make an appearance, determined to explain himself, *Ouest-France* reported, and would be giving the local journalists a long interview. Higher-ups had advised Le Bars to reconnect with his base and quash the rumors. He himself understood that to drown out talk, you had to pile more talk on top of it, that only by burying noise under more noise did you have a chance of saving your skin. He probably also thought he should have a fallback position. After all, he may just be a low-ranking cabinet minister destined to be forgotten—he might even soon be asked to return to his municipal position—the kind of person who would boast his entire life of having been a minister, or worse, of having the feeling that heaven had passed him by, a kind of holy grail in a tailored suit that only a few hundred people in the country could boast of having reached, so he would do well to stay connected to his electoral base. For that reason, striking while the iron was still hot, he had quickly scheduled his visit and alerted the local press.

9

In the clinic where Max was recovering, dawn began with a sweep of the hallways to make sure he didn't come across that day's newspaper, which of course the whole staff had read and was whispering about. To avoid any drama, the nurses had spread the word, hiding the few issues lying about in patients' rooms and break rooms, keeping an eye on Max as he walked around the flower garden, a taciturn figure under the cherry blossoms. There was even talk of increasing his dose of sedatives to detach him even further from reality, while people walked everywhere ahead of him, snatching up the newspapers. But these were the kinds of resolutions that are firmly kept for a day and then relaxed the next, especially for a daily newspaper, whose previous day's issue seemed outdated enough to have lost all its toxicity. Next day, it took just one lapse, just one copy left on a coffee table, without anyone knowing whether it was an oversight or a dirty trick by someone who might enjoy seeing Max reading the irresistible, radioactive headline THE LE BARS AFFAIR: SHE WAS POSING NAKED AT 16, with each word written in big enough letters to pierce the fog hovering around his brain and lodge like frozen daggers in the walls of his skull.

Max dropped into the nearest armchair and had the entire affair spelled out before his eyes, along with the publisher's insinuations about Laura's morals. It began to pound at the edges of his brain, the way a tinsmith might hammer a copper plate, to the point where the walls of Max's skull seemed to bulge slightly, stretching a little too far, letting in drafts and the risk of slamming doors. So the next morning, when it was time to get up and Max wasn't in his room, everybody quickly understood why.

Nobody knew what time he had escaped, and nobody made the connection with Le Bars's visit to the city. They just knew that they'd found a week's worth of drugs hidden in the hem of his pillowcase. The doctors figured that he had quietly pretended to take the drugs that were supposed to keep him calm, pretended to swallow the pill in front of the nurse and wash it down with a big glass of water, while in reality he kept it stuck under his tongue, intact, barely roughened by saliva, ready to be spit out as soon as the nurse turned her back and then hidden in the pillow. An entire week when he had pretended to be sleepy in the morning as usual, whereas in fact he remained nervous and wide awake, if that was the price to pay to keep his mind clear, if clear in this case meant the black, intractable glower we sometimes level at the world's surface, the frightening anger we experience gazing from our own darkness out basement windows at the feet of passersby moving mechanically on the sidewalk.

So nobody knew what time Max opened the window, stepped over the sill, and dropped to the lawn, quickly scaling the fence between him and the road to town, and went wandering at dawn through the empty streets of the city he knew so well. But for him, the city that day was nothing but a jumble of stones and breezes with sand and water hissing along the Sillon beach, where he slept for a few hours, exhausted from having missed too many nights, maybe including the tired counters of bars and granite facades as the body slumps at the bars' closing time. For a while, he was just a shadow in the company of lampposts, and someone finding him stretched out on the sand would scarcely believe this was the same man who two weeks earlier still reigned over the region's rings.

But here's the thing: Just because you escape from yourself doesn't mean there isn't a kind of lighthouse keeper who watches the sheets of water splashing against the windows. Somewhere inside Max, a luminous watchman still lived, serving as his compass when he awoke around eleven or noon and headed for the entrance to the casino. Not the little back door off the parking lot but the big door above the steps that he climbed before taking the central staircase up to the first floor, with the polished wooden door to Franck Bellec's office on the right.

Max didn't knock before entering, just turned the handle and gave it a sharp shove, using the natural strength that no fatigue could curb. Franck realized all this when he saw him come in and rolled backward in his chair, his hand moving toward a nearby drawer. He wasn't planning to pull out a magazine, but—like any casino manager in the world—a pistol he kept for those situations when a desperate gambler might burst into his office, the kind of person whose anger needed to be cooled by the pointing of a gun. But Franck didn't bring out his weapon. Seeing Max on the threshold looking so disheveled, neither moving nor angry, he understood that he wouldn't hurt him, barely even looked at him as his gaze ran around the room, and said, "I've come to get my gloves."

His hand still on the drawer pull, Franck glanced at the gloves under the light in the display case as Max approached them.

"Sure, I understand," he stammered. "They're yours."

Max opened the display case, took the gloves off the stand, and checked their condition, recognizing a few telltale cracks. Without a word, he tied them together by their laces, gave Bellec a dull look, and went out. As he watched Max leave, it's possible that Franck understood what was going to happen, but he let the thought pass through him without the least desire to stop him, as if he were discovering a kind of inner peace in this new passivity, which he may even have found surprising. In any case, nobody stopped Max from descending the big central staircase, with his gloves tied together and bouncing at arm's length. Nobody, not even Hélène, who earlier, from the shadow of the bar counter, had watched him climb the stairs, deliberately letting him go up to her brother's office and catch him there. As she watched Max cross the hall in the other direction, she may have tried to approach him, but, as she said later, "He wasn't seeing me." So all she thought to do later, after Max quickly went outside, as she watched him against the backdrop of the sea, which was more pictorial than usual, all she thought to do, as I said, was to call Laura and tell her, "Look, your father is about to do something stupid," though today we can still argue whether what he was going to do, as if it were written on a banner being flown over the city, was really stupid.

10

For a brain-damaged man, Max still had his sense of timing. At the very moment he was leaving the casino hall, Quentin Le Bars was stepping off of the TGV that had brought him from Paris, greeted at the end of the platform by a crowd of reporters in a holiday mood, who clustered around to accompany him to the Neptune. He had asked them to come to the big room reserved especially for the occasion so he could tell them how happy he was to be there, and to apologize that circumstances forced him to spend a moment on the sordid affair that had wounded him so deeply, yes, so deeply. Heaving a heavy sigh, he spent a solid hour pulling out all the stops, displaying his good faith like a long parchment under a flurry of questions he could have written himself, since they nearly all boosted his attempts to win his audience's understanding. He didn't deny that in a moment of weakness he had succumbed and allowed himself to be seduced by a young woman who came on to him so artfully and persistently. But as for the rest, "I won't let anyone claim that..." etc., etc.

Besides, Le Bars asked the Neptune audience, was there a single document proving that he had ever helped her get any housing? There wasn't, for the good reason that he had never taken the slightest step to help her—as Laura would discover later. He hadn't even mentioned her to the city housing authority. "I have never liked special favors or backroom deals," he said, enunciating slowly and carefully, to be sure it would be printed word for word in the newspaper, buoyed by that frightening, unnerving strength that some men have of lying without blinking. And when one reporter, a little sharper than the rest, asked him to explain how Laura Le Corre wound up working for Franck Bellec, he didn't bat an eyelash. The fact that Franck, who still saw himself as the minister's right arm, was standing just few yards away, didn't keep Le Bars from saying, "You know, when you're the mayor, you have to deal with people as you find them. That doesn't mean that you approve of their activities."

In a single swivel of necks, everyone in the room turned to Bellec, searching his face for the sign of the slap he had just received. Everyone, that is, except Le Bars, who calmly waited for the next question. And when the same reporter asked, "Are you suggesting that some of Mr. Bellec's activities aren't quite legal?" the room not only kept its unanimous, concerned gaze on Bellec, it began to echo with a background hum of many voices that made its way very slowly through the gathered crowd, a rumble of surprise rising like a neume in the nave of a cathedral that was cut short by the mayor's voice.

"I should remind you that I am the minister of maritime affairs," he said solemnly, "not the head of the vice squad."

Le Bars probably imagined that his friend Bellec would understand the situation, given that the two were so used to each other as to know that blows struck in public don't count, being the theatrical and necessarily rigged version of their dark connivance. But if he had taken the time to catch Franck's eye at that moment, if he hadn't blithely picked up the thread of his speech and invited the crowd to meet him at the marina in an hour, he would have realized that Franck Bellec did not understand this at all.

Le Bars ended the questioning and left the little stage that had been set up for him, followed out by a cohort of reporters keeping pace, like a wedding cortege after mass, and you could almost imagine one of them throwing rice at him. But the groom left a little quicker than he might have on a Saturday outside the church and got into his car, with no white dress next to him, only the new mayor—his former deputy—and told the new chauffeur to drive them to the marina. New, that is, because Max Le Corre wasn't driving, of course. And it wasn't Max Le Corre who watched Le Bars in his rearview mirror, looking for his smile or his complicity. Sitting in his usual place on the same leather seat, Le Bars couldn't help but think about Max, couldn't help but feel his breath as the car drove through the old city and along the ramparts, perhaps spotting pieces of the posters announcing the great lost fight on a wall or the base of a lamppost, scraps shredded by rain and wind but still showing Max's dark stare, washed out and distorted by the wet paper.

But who at that moment would take the time to see how closely the image resembled its model? I mean how many of those outdated shrouds still carried in their very rips such an intimate picture of the real Max? At that hour he was still wandering the streets of the city, his face as wrinkled as the outdated poster, his French champion gloves swinging along with his steps, seemingly leading him aimlessly down long paved alleyways, waving his arms in strange ways, shadowboxing the empty, unresponsive air, noticed only by passersby who occasionally turned around to briefly smile at this eccentric, this harmless loony, the way people used to look kindly on an escapee from the Petites Maisons asylum. But Max wasn't seeing anyone. His only adversaries were the thousands of invisible insects buzzing around him, as if his only thought was a cloud of flies accompanying him at every step, drawn by the warmth of his face, flitting a few inches from his skin, while no waving of his arms could drive them off, no fist nor left hook could stop this infinite, agitated, and random deployment of all those idea-flies, which weren't assailing him—the expression would be too fine—but rather taunting him without really taking a fixed shape, to the point where one could wonder if that would ever happen.

"Actually, it would be better if it didn't take a fixed shape," the doctor had told Laura several times as they watched Max on the clinic's garden walkways, passing mute and agitated along the iron fence, both of them resigned to the idea of never seeing him in his right mind again. It should be said that it wasn't really a thing that appeared from one hour to the next but that had inflated and swollen in silence, like a plastic film that gradually came unstuck from its support, and then one day, helium or something similar pulled it toward the sky, and it began to float in the air. Something that can't be named had moved off and taken flight, had begun to whirl above him and spiral off in curves and arabesques. The doctor continued: "Sometimes the brain is like a kite that lifts you by the feet and suspends you in the air, upside down."

Laura had plenty of time to think about all this as she sat in the passenger seat of a car prowling the city's outskirts with the ancient queen of the night who had alerted her at the wheel. The two women agreed that they had to do something, find Max before it was too late. They crisscrossed the neighborhoods as slowly as a police patrol car, both staying open to every hypothesis until settling on the most likely one: that to find Max, they had to find Le Bars.

11

Mayors attend inaugurations, art openings, and official ceremonies at the steady tempo of someone saying the rosary, events that everyone has a good reason for attending, without quite knowing what brought them there. Today, a small crowd was already waiting on the old stone piers above the inner marinas and their brand-new docks. It included officials and the merely curious, with a large number of sailors who'd come to admire the new infrastructure where they could finally moor their boats, discussing the results of the construction while awaiting the minister's imminent arrival, keeping one eye on the water and one on the road leading to the esplanade. Others had come to greet a man they practically considered a relative, as happens when a mayor rises in rank: Every city resident feels they now have the ear of someone in power. In the time since Le Bars was appointed minister, you'd never heard so many "Yes, I know him very well" and "I went to school with him," as each person stuffed their personal beliefs deep into their pockets and came hoping to get a handshake, which struck them as the very least consideration they could aspire to, already worried that the prestigious minister might fail to give them what they felt they deserved. This anxiety was soon lifted by the arrival of the black car, from which the new mayor stepped out first, followed by Minister Le Bars, who deliberately played up the casualness of his bearing and the godlike confidence he was able to exude for the cameras recording the event, that is, filming the assembled voters' predictable wonder at this great investment which, as the minister had remarked earlier, reminded everyone of the city's maritime heritage, unreeling long sentences jotted down on the corner of a table by some well-exercised bureaucrat, one for the city's glorious past, another for its glorious future, and between them, the glorious present we were now living—a marvelous time synthesis in which the Republic was invoked hundreds of times each day in front of some wall or fence synonymous with progress and communal life.

But in matters of communal life, one person had long since dropped out, and that was Max Le Corre. Now stationed on the other side of the road at some distance from the event, he could follow the ceremony's orchestrated movements while hidden behind the cars parked in the shadow of the ramparts. The scene looked like the backdrop of a theater stage, in which Max was a main character preparing in the wings, his muscular body standing out against the stony gray setting in a way no attentive spectator could miss, and who, as we know, would upset everything in his path. As it happens, that attentive spectator was already present, looking at the black stripes of Max's tracksuit between two cars, or maybe his shaved skull above the car roofs. And no one would be surprised to learn that said spectator, likewise standing apart from the crowd, was named Franck Bellec, still smarting from the humiliation he had suffered an hour ago, but also still standing and intent on proving it. And Franck looked at Max. And Max looked at Franck. And it was as if each knew what the other would do or not do. As if Bellec knew he wasn't going to save Le Bars this time, and Max knew it too, knew that Franck, motionless in his white suit and taut with impatience at the thought of what he sensed was going to happen, would no more stir than a spectator in the balcony at an opera. At that moment, in their sustained exchange of looks, you would have said that together they were erasing the black years that had separated them. Watching Max bare his chest in the cool April air, Franck would have accompanied him into the ring if he could.

Because in Max's head, it was a ring, of course. In Max's head this was a real fight, and they would soon call his name to cheer him and lead him in to face his opponent of the day, the fearsome Quentin Le Bars, brought specially from Paris to challenge him in his city. Soon he would drape the big robe with his embroidered name over the chair, and the two would size up each other's bodies before the first bell, as usual, appraising each other with the same prolonged, animal pride, like two old lions who had each so far managed to keep their territories, challenging each other indirectly by threats without actual confrontation, but who were now prepared to have it out in front of everybody. I should say this was only happening in Max's and Franck's telepathic minds, not in that of Le Bars, who just then was stepping out of the limousine, or in the earpieces of the two men in black who for some time had been x-raying the surroundings with their robotic eyes, in case some lunatic tried to attack the security of the state—you never know.

So either they didn't see the man steadying himself with a hand against the wall as he pulled off his tracksuit pants, or they didn't think he was a lunatic. Either way, they didn't view him as a threat, a man who some recognized as the defeated boxer they had admired, but most figured he was one of the inevitable quantum of oddballs who show up at every public gathering. Still hidden behind the cars, in the makeshift locker room he'd created, Max was now pulling on his gloves one by one, and bouncing in place to keep from cooling off before hearing his name and walking down the imaginary hallway that would open for him onto the central square. For the time being, however, the only imaginary hallway was opening for Le Bars. Flanked by the two colossi with white earpieces, he moved through the little compressed mass of bystanders, shaking all those previously anxious hands that were now assured of his undying friendship. He then climbed the few steps to the stage that had been built with scaffolding, creating a kind of shaky dais on the pier's uneven stones, having asked his bodyguards to stay below and not accompany him, because he was in his city and it mattered that he remain "close to the people," as people in his position are in the habit of saying. Now that he was elevated a couple of yards, it was time to recognize a few officials who were impatient to have their turn onstage: the harbormaster and the local elected officials who couldn't miss such an opportunity to welcome a minister.

And this time it wasn't Quentin Le Bars speaking to them but the minister of maritime affairs. Quentin himself was more than happy to lend his body to the other man, the minister, sloughing off the weight of the sad affair that had so tarnished him, by wrapping himself in his national persona, promptly erasing the affair through the magical, whitening effect of his immunity. Draped in the robes of his position, as it were, Le Bars had no way of suspecting that the crowd held a few people who saw him not as a minister, mayor, or official of any kind but only as "that bastard Le Bars," nor could that bastard Le Bars suspect the angry energy he generated here and there, and which was now flooding Max's nerves, the nerves of a father well aware that he wasn't the real offended party, but who was probably the only person who could restore the balance of those ancient scales that so often tip toward the powerful.

For all we know, the same thoughts occurred to Laura, riding in Hélène's car, as the local radio station announced Le Bars's arrival at the marina, and they caused her to turn to Hélène and say, "Le Bars and the marina! That's where he went!" Hélène took the first right and raced for the harbor in the distance behind the barriers, but the cops had cordoned off the event, forcing them to park some distance away. They quickly got out of the car and started running toward the esplanade, which Laura saw less as a ring than an arena because of the unfairness of the fight for Max, that solitary gladiator, a sorry Spartacus whose only potential followers were laughter and pity.

But that Spartacus wasn't expecting them, and Max, his gloves laced, stepped out from behind the cars as Franck watched, and Franck, who knew him so well, suspected that at that moment he was concentrating hard, ready to fight the thirty-seventh and final bout of his long career, refereed by the ships' masts rising above the pier.

So that was it. On the dais, the harbormaster introduced his guest and said what an honor it was for the local boating community to have its minister visit. At the mic stand that was raised for him, Le Bars in turn thanked the harbormaster and began, as was appropriate, to go down the official list of people he wanted to thank, that is, the litany of titles of the people around him—"Mr. Mayor," "Mr. General Counsel"—while Max slipped like an eel through the sparse ranks of the people listening. They hardly noticed the man dressed like a boxer passing by them, or rather they saw him clearly but went on acting as if that wasn't the most important thing that was happening, all mesmerized by Le Bars's amplified voice bouncing off the fences. They may also have felt that nothing bad could happen with all the cops and men in black stationed around the esplanade. "Mr. President of the Sports Commission," "Mr. Regional Council Vice President" continued as Max got close to the few metal steps up to the stage, maybe hoping that among the titles Le Bars was stringing like pearls, he might hear his own, "Champion of France." But no, instead of that, there was "Mr. Regional Councillor" and "Mr. Director of Municipal Services," "Ladies and gentlemen deputies," and finally, "My dear fellow citizens." Le Bars took a breath before launching into the body of his speech, but he barely had time to say "I" or "I am" when he noticed or sensed the crowd's entire attention suddenly shift, a hundred gazes concentrated in a single beam focused on Max's bare-chested body. He had burst onto the stage, having practically bounded up the four steps from the ground, rising the way an ancient god might emerge from the sea—Neptune in the flesh, but raising his old, ill-laced gloves to eye level instead of a trident. Bouncing on the balls of his feet, he cast a momentary lost look over the crowd, an undifferentiated mass in which he couldn't recognize a single face, not even that of his own daughter, who was now making her way through it. Laura was tempted to cry out, but afraid that any word might electrify the situation, as the officials on the stage backed away from the boxer's threatening gloves—nobody wants to catch a stray bullet from a shootout. And Le Bars immediately grasped what was happening, just fast enough to think of his bodyguards and wonder what the hell they were doing, as he was rushed by a madman who thought he was in a boxing ring.

For Le Bars, this was certainly no ring but rather a little fortress deserted by its chain-mailed guards and whose gate he had become, attacked by a battering ram. And Max, who knew all about battering, now threw his full weight at a petrified Le Bars, his right fist slamming into the man's jaw as the left crushed and bloodied his nose, sending him backward against the barriers that kept him from tumbling into the harbor, and then promptly collapsing on the ground, dazed by Max's powerful blows, as the men in black watched, too late.

Maybe they thought it was a terrorist attack, because it had erupted out of nowhere, a grain of sand falling into the gears and disrupting the smooth running of a powerful, discreet, and self-sufficient world—and what could a grain of sand mean to the two colossi who hadn't seen anything coming? Just a grain of sand in a set of gears that normally turned without the slightest hitch, except that this time, as they now realized, it was much more than a grain of sand—the whole edifice of their castle was collapsing into itself. And their castle wasn't some delicate house of cards but rather dungeons and arrow slits, and if someone managed to cross the moats, every wall held crossbowmen and vats of boiling oil ready to rain down on any lunatic trying to get in. Which is what happened. Not a vat of oil or a flaming arrow, but a pair of trained guys in black who were annoyed they couldn't have intervened sooner or noticed Max climbing so agilely. One of them decided not to bother thinking any further. If his weapon was ever going to serve in his lifetime, the moment was obviously now, to save not only the minister but the whole castle whose perimeter had been breached. He pulled the gun from his belt, held it out at arm's length, and yelled, "Don't move! Don't move, or I'll shoot!"

That was the sentence Laura heard when she reached the foot of the dais, forced to raise her head to see the man pointing his weapon at her boxer father. Max meanwhile continued punching Le Bars, demanding that he stand up and continue the fight, while the bodyguard feverishly repeated, "Don't move! I'm telling you, don't move!" But Max wasn't listening, didn't hear the guard's words as they overlapped with those of his daughter, who was now shouting, "Stop, Dad, stop!" Finally, he straightened up, leaving a motionless Le Bars dazed, turned to face the man in black, and advanced toward him, hopping from foot to foot, his gloves still raised, as if the fight couldn't end, as if the kite that served as his mind had gotten snagged in the branches of a tree high in the skies, and some infernal goddess was snickering as she pulled on the strings. Max kept hopping and rolling his fists, taunting the man pointing his weapon at arm's length, "Come on, come closer," while Laura screamed, "Stop! Stop!" until the two bodyguards, still wearing the earpieces that made them look like androids, finally realized that the man in shorts who dreamed he was still boxing, the man who had just broken a minister's nose, was nothing but a nut job, a practically harmless weirdo, and that between the two of them they could neutralize him without violence, at least in the way they acted nonviolently, by each taking one of his arms, twisting it behind his back, forcing him to kneel, and saying, "Shut up now, okay? Shut up!"

Laura would have liked to join Max at that moment, would have wanted to be arrested as well, have her arm twisted, be told to shut up. But she was powerless, pushed away from the foot of the steps by the quickly assembled cordon of police that surged forward en masse to disperse the crowd, and could only watch the scene of her father's arrest, still on his knees at the firm command of the two guards, who knew they would be fired before the end of the day. Peering between a pair of cops blocking her way, she tried to catch her father's eye, dying to share a look with him. But Max Le Corre, his head pinned to the ground by the rougher of the two guards, was no longer there, was somewhere up in a boxing pantheon, maybe between Joe Louis and Mike Tyson.

As the crowd gradually thinned, Laura was joined by Hélène, who gave a last look at her brother, a white figure walking toward the casino, serene and indemnified. A minister still lay up in the ring lost against the western sky, and Franck had time to read in Le Bars's battered face the price paid for that indemnity like a label on a piece of clothing. But in this story, Bellec is a secondary character. When Le Bars was helped to his feet by the few deputies still with him, and managed to descend the four steps that brought him down to our level, he didn't try to avoid looking at Laura, who stood there, erect, her eyes locked on his, as if wanting to tell him one last time that it wasn't over, and that for her, it would never be over. But all she received by way of an answer, all she got from the bloody handkerchief Le Bars was holding over his nose, was the look he gave her: dull, indolent, and almost impenetrable.

Max Le Corre was sentenced to two years in prison for assaulting a person vested with public authority and for threatening state security. Laura Le Corre's complaint was dismissed without further action.

TANGUY VIEL was born in Brest in 1973. He is the author of several novels, including *The Absolute Perfection of Crime*, winner of the Prix Fénéon and the Prix littéraire de la vocation; *Beyond Suspicion*; *The Disappearance of Jim Sullivan*; and *Article 353* (Other Press, 2019). He lives near Orléans, France.

WILLIAM RODARMOR has translated some forty-five books and screenplays in genres ranging from literary fiction to espionage and fantasy. His recent translations include Tanguy Viel's *Article 353* and Nicolas Mathieu's *And Their Children After Them*, for which he won the 2021 Albertine Prize. He lives in Berkeley, California.